PRAISE FOR THE NATURAL ENGINES SERIES

"Enchanting, mysterious, and strange, *A Palace Near the Wind* is a heartbreaking story of homecoming and self-discovery. Combining the best of folklore and science fiction, this eco-narrative on human greed and superhuman hope is not to be missed."

KRITIKA H. RAO, author of *The Surviving Sky*

"A fantastic and magical tale of survival and rebellion set against the backdrop of a struggle between nature and the forces of industry. Ai Jiang has written a beautiful and all too-fitting story that resonates with the choices we face in our times."

P. DJÈLÍ CLARK, author of *The Dead Cat Tail Assassins* and *A Master of Djinn*

"A breathtakingly imagined story of ecological disaster, torn families, betrayal, and hope. Unlike anything I've ever read before—like Ghibli retelling Tolkien through Chinese myth—with tree-like deities, political intrigue, wind magic, and mecha. Utterly enchanting."

A.Y. CHAO, author of *Shanghai Immortal*

"Beautifully written and intricately layered, this novella is part fairy tale and part tale of rebellion and hope. A compelling and complex story of court politics, hidden secrets, sacrifices, alliances, and characters fighting for their freedom."

A.C. WISE, author of *Wendy, Darling* and *Hooked*

"Haunting and lovely, Jiang creates a world of wonder in *A Palace Near the Wind*. Your heart will break as Lufeng must give up her home, her beliefs, and her sense of family. You'll root for her as she builds her courage to forge a new future for herself, and those precious to her."

JULIA VEE, co-author of The Phoenix Hoard trilogy

"Elegant and otherworldly. A tale of family and duty, devotion and obligation – and the shattering secrets hidden in every past. A glorious new myth from a talented new voice."

A.G. SLATTER, author of *All the Murmuring Bones* and *The Briar Book of the Dead*

"A beautiful, heart-rending parable about the ways grief and loss feed on the vitality of the living, eventually making ghosts of us all."

GARETH L. POWELL, author of *Stars and Bones* and *Future's Edge*

Also by Ai Jiang
and available from Titan Books

A Palace Near the Wind

A RIVER FROM the SKY

AI JIANG

TITAN BOOKS

A River From the Sky
Print edition ISBN: 9781803369525
Inkstone edition ISBN: 9781835419212
Broken Binding edition ISBN: 9781835419229
E-book edition ISBN: 9781803369532

Published by Titan Books
A division of Titan Publishing Group Ltd
144 Southwark Street, London SE1 0UP
www.titanbooks.com

First edition: April 2026
10 9 8 7 6 5 4 3 2 1

A CIP catalogue record for this title is available from the British Library.

EU RP (for authorities only)
eucomply OÜ, Pärnu mnt. 139b-14, 11317 Tallinn, Estonia
hello@eucompliancepartner.com, +3375690241

Printed and bound in Great Britain by CPI Group (UK) Ltd, Croydon, CR0 4YY.

To those who breathe hope
into the generations to come

GLOSSARY

Geography

Feng: a region of forests, streams, and wildlife that is the home of Wind Walkers.

Glace: a region of waterfalls, lakes, and rivers that is the home of Water Shifters.

Clay: a desert-like region that is predominantly made up of markets and roaming tradespeople.

The Palaces: made of bone, stone, and metal, encased in the wall that separates Feng, Glace, and Clay from Gear and Engine. The Palaces serve as gates between the two sides of the wall.

Gear: an island which is composed of water wheels and wind churners that are powered by Currents.

The Eternal Bridges: three tracks that connect the island of Gear and Engine, resembling conveyer belts.

Engine: an iron giant with a seemingly endless number of chambers both within and without that house the Cogs, approximately fifty stories in height.

Natural Engines

Wind Walkers: the people of Feng with bark skin, needle thread hair, and branched limbs, with the ability to borrow wind.

Water Shifters: the people of Glace whose bodies are entirely made of contained water, rippling through like endless streams, with the ability to shift water.

Natural Titans

Orics: a combination of Water Shifters and the substance called oric (a type of corrosive acid).

Currents: a combination of Wind Walkers and Water Shifters with affinities for both wind and water.

Sun Cores: alchemized versions of Wind Walkers who have undergone a first death through burning.

Humans

Land Wanderers: the humans who live in Clay.

Cogs: the humans who live in Engine.

THE BURIED ENGINE

They called her a tamed disaster, a smothered storm, a settled earthquake, a droughted flood, a stilled eruption, stifled wind—The Buried Engine.

I want to tell you of the time I asked the Buried Engine—

Who came first?

Her response—

Hm. A version of us, and a version of them.

Many might not have realized, but the palaces began as places of worship, of religion and faith.

I—

Worship?

She—

Yes.

Everything they had ever created was with
the image of the natural gods in mind,
as an attempt to become more like them, us.

I—

We? Gods?

She—

Yes.

Can I tell you something?

I—

Yes.

She—

I saw a future where scattered
onyx dropped like acid rain.

I saw a future where the world was
consumed by a different kind of fire outside
of flames, one driven by wind and moisture.

I saw a future where all our homes remained

as they once were, and then... one where
nothing remained, one where there were
roots splintered, severed, bodies evaporating
and turning to steam to join the clouds in
the sky, the natural becoming the unnatural
and the unnatural becoming natural.

What if you had to destroy one thing to save
another? How would you make that choice?

You cannot save everyone. There
will always be sacrifices—the question
is not when, nor how, but who?

I have seen all the endings, and it seems
every one of them leads to a single conclusion.

Yet, every dead thing can be reborn,
rise from the ashes, and for as long as we
are living, we can continue to struggle
to survive—for as long as we can.

But wouldn't it be wonderful if we
didn't have to wait for death to realize that
the blades that drew blood were held
within our own hands this entire time?

I—

Then, what do you find in this
life that is worth living for?

She—

Sometimes it cannot be placed into words,
but all of it, all of it is worth living, and I want to
cherish every breath that leaves and enters, and
sensation and experience, every life and death.

I would love to witness for myself, and with
all of you, and revel in the fruits of your glory
and wither in the destruction of your wars and
hope that beneath it all, the seeds of hope will
continue to sprout from beneath trampled
soils, may persist to grow, bloom, scatter,
and take root where it is seemingly barren.

And I shall remain, as long as all of
you do, because there can only be gods if
there are those who believe and worship
them, or else they are nothing at all.

1

LUFENG
THE OTHER SIDE

Terrified, I swayed atop unpredictable waves, buoyant, if precariously, in a body that was not my own.

My younger siblings nestled against me, anxious—my youngest sister Chuiliu, slenderer than I remember her to be, more so than my youngest brother Changqing, only half Chuiliu's size, legs dangling rather than pressed against the floor of the Traveler, whose expression was much calmer, almost sleepy, too young to understand our precarious situation. On the other side of the Traveler was the Water Shifter Geyser, first my Palace instructor, then ally, now somehow savior. Only half lucid, he shook his head, and the glaze in his eyes melted away to alertness as the rippling currents that ran under the translucence of his skin stuttered occasionally rather than running unhalted.

It was a miracle we had survived the fall from the heights of the Palace. When I turned back to look upwards, though there was a gaping cavern where the floor-to-ceiling window to Mother's room once sat, no one stood watching from its opening.

In the distance, divided by the stretch of the sea and its turbulent waves, stood a giant. Its metal body shone with a dull glow under the sunless skies; a thin layer of smog hung in the air. Upon its head there was a large turning wheel, and water tumbled down the sides with gentle grace into the sea below—a river from the sky.

Yet, the beauty of the endless stream did not distract from what seemed to be plaguing the giant, who was known as Engine. Settled atop the flattened peak of a low mountain, the iron behemoth crawled with what appeared to be decaying copper festering upwards like clawing veins, spidering metallic fingers, like a disease eating at the roots of a tree and its branches that took the form of tiny, colorful bulb protrusions staggering up the length of the walls. For a moment, these bulbs appeared like rain bloom seeds, waiting to scatter, but instead stuck, withering.

"Corroveins," Geyser murmured as he followed my gaze toward Engine. "That is what Wind Walkers and Water Shifters refer to them as. The humans that live on the iron giant—the Cogs—call it 'rust.' Or at least, an alchemized mutation of it created by the rebels."

"Mutation?" I asked.

"Like me, now, like... Changqing," was Geyser's response. My brother stared up at the Water Shifter, head tilted to the side.

Titans. *Natural Titans.* Geyser had explained that that's what both he and Changqing had become after entering Zinc's experimental chambers. Changqing's new ability to shift water, along with the capacity to borrow wind, made him a *Current.* Perhaps it was his new affinity to water that made him so unafraid of the relentless violence of the waves as they bombarded our Traveler.

I stared at the way the flow of water that made up Geyser's body shifted differently than before—thick, dense, rather than free-flowing. For a moment, Geyser seemed to shrink away from my gaze. But the slight tremor was brief. "Oric," he said. He did not explain further.

Between us, adrift in the dysfunctional Traveler, and the iron giant sat the island known as Gear. Scattered across it were enormous wheels, dense and collected like the unnatural trees of a Land Wanderer-constructed forest, turning by the force of wind and water. Shadows slipped past with each turn, but I did not stare too hard because my pores tightened uncomfortably at the thought. Perhaps it was better not to know what those shadows were.

I looked away, past the wheels. Peeking from between them, on the other side of the island, three long stretches of metal connected the island of Gear and the iron giant of Engine. The stretches of metal shifted forward at a steady pace both towards and away from the island and the iron giant. Beneath the belts sat wheel-like mechanisms, propelling the metal belts forward. There were occasional stutters in the rhythm of movement, much like the way the Travelers' movements were sometimes jerky rather than smooth.

Chuiliu withdrew towards me, as though physically shuddering away from Engine as we floated closer.

"It will be alright," I whispered into her needle threads, but I was not sure if my words were truth.

In contrast, Changqing leant forward, as though drawn towards the iron giant.

As we approached, at times, I caught glimpses of who I assumed were the Cogs upon slated, protruding rooftops from the side of Engine. Geyser told us that compared to the people of Clay, the Land Wanderers, the Cogs were reliant on the controlled interior of Engine: inside the metal giant, the environment was held at a steady temperature, shielded from the turbulence of weather, rain and storm, extreme heat or cold. The Cogs had weak bodies, making them susceptible to illness and death. It would be difficult for them to live the way Wind Walkers and Water Shifters did—among trees, floating in water.

A ping came from inside Geyser's robe. When he pulled out a comscreen, he showed me a message from Sangshu. Beneath I saw an unfamiliar name attached to Geyser's response. The content of the messages escaped me as I instead fixated on the name that did not match the only one I knew.

"Exile Song?" I murmured.

Geyser looked up.

"Yes..." he whispered. "My name. My true name. From Glace. Home. Or at least the verbalized Script version."

I wanted to ask, *What is your name in Song?* but before I could, Geyser—Exile Song—had already moved on, and the quiet moment was lost. There was a part of me that wanted to grasp it again, linger within it, ask and have my ask be answered. I held myself back. This was not the time.

"Sangshu will meet us," he said, then paused, as though contemplating his next words.

In the flurry of the fall and the chaos of the moment of escape, I had completely forgotten about my sister. My breath quickened, and I could feel the wind collecting in a gentle pool around me and my siblings at the thought of seeing my fourth sister again. Though I knew Sangshu had broken away from Zinc's control, I could not help but latch onto the scorn from my other sisters, Heshi and Yunshu, when I pleaded for their aid and had been cruelly denied. But the thoughts flew from my mind as quickly as a passing breeze at Geyser's next words.

"Don't be alarmed by her appearance when you see her," he said without meeting my eyes.

"Her appearance?" I asked.

"She may look... different from how you remember her."

Heshi and Yunshu returned to my mind, their sanded complexions, along with Father's. A shudder rippled through me, and my fingers curled—rough bark against rough bark, fingers scraping palm.

This time, instead of Chuiliu being the one clutching on, it was I who clung to her slender arm, and she seemed to take on the role of comforter, patting a hand soothingly against my forearm. I did not want to show her weakness, but I was also glad for her strength. She should be back in Feng. Safe. Not here. I took her hand in mine, then nudged Changqing away from the floating Traveler's edge as he tried to lean further over its side

2

SANGSHU

ONE ANNUAL AND SIX CYCLES AGO

Meet me in five revolutions of the Time Teller, I told Exile Song, *in case it is the last time we ever meet.* Though at the time, Exile Song was loyal to Copper and I to Zinc, he was the closest thing to a friend I had during my mostly isolated apprenticeship.

I took my notes for the alchemy of Sun Cores from Zinc's desk—an imposing stump scarred with designs of intricate alchemy symbols and light indenting from where Zinc had pressed too hard with a quill—which sat in front of the alchemy chamber at the back of the library as though standing guard.

I wanted my alchemy to be a surprise for Zinc. To show him what I could accomplish on my own.

I had been so confident before stepping into Zinc's

library. The alchemy experiment chamber sat, looming, at the back of the room, with the two floor-to-ceiling shelving units lining its sides. Staring at the chamber now wavered my resolve.

What was worse, being burned dead or alive? Being cut down first, or feeling the moment your end arrives?

But there wasn't time to dwell.

I peeled off my white cloak, then the white robes beneath, exposing the bark of my body with a shudder as cold air sliced down my back, then I opened the smooth iron door of the chamber. A wave of heat consumed my face to the verge of splintering the bark. Every pore tightened, like scorpion pincers pinching, a bombardment of stings from its tail prying at my flesh, my skin withdrew from the onslaught in uncontrollable flinches.

I knew Zinc and all his guards were still at the Palace, on the other side of the wall. Even if he were to see the smoke, he wouldn't be alarmed. Experiments were common. After all, that was why he took me in as an apprentice.

I entered the chamber, shut the door behind me, and hoped by the end I'd be lucid enough to step out.

The iron interior of the chamber was scarred with soot and the remaining saliva of fire. Though there was at least a wind's breath of space between me and the curved walls, I felt closed in, the air growing dense, a rapid compression, the beginnings of an excruciating suffocation. I imagined the dead driftwood burning beneath its exterior, and my decomposition was quick to ignite—layer by layer my bark burned, peeling back all that I was and had been.

Searing.

But before I perished, the ashes from my skin began to reattach to my body like armor, relayering what had been unlayered, and the dead core of my wooden heart began to melt, simmer, becoming a collected inferno within the now-hardened chamber. The minutiae of my alchemical transformation took the form of a rebuilding, a painful weight, like being crushed beneath boulder upon boulder until my limbs ached under the pressure of an ancient mountain and a thousand needles holding my body still from collapse. Yet, I refused to allow a single shout of pain escape, no matter the gruesome cruelty of the flame's continuing sear.

Then, behind the lids of closed eyes, I saw the Palace. The first time I entered. Its coldness. Its desolation.

The first time I stepped onto the warm sands of Clay's terracotta dunes, bare feet sinking.

The ceremony that took place in the filled yet empty Palace dining hall, that was not the anticipated marriage to the king but instead the proposal of an apprenticeship I eagerly took. I placed my hand in Zinc's the way a daughter would take her father's guiding hand, and back then he seemed far more like family than the father I had never known. And because Zinc had looked at me in a way that no other being had ever done so before: he saw me as someone with potential.

Within the blaze of the chamber, I was becoming something more powerful—quicker than the storm of winds, stronger than the unrelenting currents of water, something that burnt longer than wood. It was what Zinc wished to create, and now, *I* had. Every breath, instead of cool, revitalizing air, was a sharp, dry inferno that scraped at the walls of my throat—like nails digging.

Close to losing consciousness, through the buzzing of flames which resembled the sound of crickets during desert midnights, I heard the door of the chamber being pried open. I immediately collapsed forth in the rush of coolness that I never thought I'd feel again, and into the arms of a being whose skin felt almost frigid to my inferno.

Exile Song.

Many were born struggling to stay alive. I was born ready to die. That had been the last thought I had as I stepped into the alchemy chamber. But I forgot this as soon as I tumbled out, limbs aching, with the sensation of every crevice that had broken across my surface prying open, ripping at their edges, wider and wider.

The last thing I saw through bleary eyes was Exile Song's grimace.

No.

It wasn't my vision.

It was steam.

Accompanied by a constant, merciless and violent heat trailing upwards from the arm that held onto me tight and refused to let go.

But in my mind, only one thought remained. *Are you proud of me, mentor?*

3

SANGSHU
THE LIBRARY, NOW

In front of me were the floor-to-ceiling glass doors of the library, which nested at the summit of Engine right next to the waterfall of the Time Teller. An alchemy lock, like a mosaic of intricate iron puzzle pieces hovering at chest height, stood between me and the interior—one that only unsealed at the touch of Zinc's skin.

I bent down and drew within me the simmering fountain of inferno tears until a searing breath left my lips, turned the iron lock amber, scarlet, cerulean, before melting it away altogether. There was no alarm to trigger, for Zinc had always trusted his alchemy more than anything else in his world.

I made my way to Zinc's desk and stared down at the papers scattered across its surface. His version of Sun

Core alchemy, carefully detailed and corrupted, was marked up with endless questions demanding why his own experiments had yet to succeed. His tireless efforts over the annual or so since my escape amazed me.

Zinc had once asked me, *Are you willing to die for creation?*

At that moment, how alike we'd become was both unexpected, yet also not quite unexpected, even given the brief time I'd been following in his footsteps—until I surpassed him, until I was leaving my own, without ever once looking back, without realizing how those very steps had been burning the path I walked the entire time.

Until now.

Zinc's ambition and stubbornness were both his greatest virtues and his most tragic shortcomings, coupled with an intelligence that was as impressive as it was threatening.

Almost two annuals prior, I was close to discovering how I could alchemize myself into a Sun Core. I knew it was a secret I would be able to hide from Zinc forever even after my success. Because to become a Sun Core, I had to first willingly die, take my decay and layer it with stone—a process I so carefully set up. Those were the easiest steps of the long and enduring procedure. It was something I knew Zinc would never be willing to do, to tear himself down then put himself back together, to *die*. He clutched at survival, desperately, even though he tried not to show it. All those who came before him had done the same. And perhaps that was the one thing that was predictable about this unpredictable being who the Cogs called the Iron Alchemist, some with reverence, others with scorn.

Within me were the carefully contained collected tears of the sun, simmering in their glorious amber, like wine in a vessel. Zinc desperately craved to have them at his own disposal, to fuel Engine for eternity. The first time I'd wept after the alchemy of flesh I'd performed on myself, I'd evaporated Exile Song's entire arm, because the tears within me did not only leak from my eyes but out from every fissure and crevice across my body.

With a deep breath, I willed the tears of the sun at my core, where the heartwood once sat, to rise, to move upwards towards my arm, down to my hand. As the tears collected at my fingertips, I picked up the notes for his corrupted version of my Sun Core alchemy. In my hands, the scroll quickly disintegrated until it was nothing but ashes fluttering onto the ground. I would not allow him to create more than he already had. I then spotted his failed plans to turn Walkers and Shifters into Land Wanderers and Cogs like himself, in hope that it may reveal how to perform the reverse. That remained unsuccessful because he'd only managed to change their appearances but not their roots nor crests. I thought of Father, his face sanded down, blanched, a towering ghost, shrouded in silks. I burned those documents, too.

This small, futile victory filled me with both an eager anticipation and unpent anger. The feeling shook me, because of how it was likened to the fervent zeal Zinc himself had expressed every time something went his way—whether it was a certain plan or a new discovery he was keen to show off. I was unwilling to admit to the impact Zinc had had on me because it would mean acknowledging the power of his influence.

I spent endless hours within this library as his apprentice, this library that was once accessible to the rest of Engine, long before Zinc, but now made inaccessible—its contents seen as archaic and dangerous unless they were in the hands of the Iron Alchemist, who could do no wrong. Occasionally, they'd allowed apprentices peeks at these precious secrecies, but only if what we learned benefited those like Zinc, only if what we learned wouldn't surpass them, only if what we learned were the things they wished for us to learn and nothing more.

Much like the master alchemists who came before Zinc, Zinc was first proud, then spiteful, at the fact I'd accomplished something he himself hadn't. He began seeing me as a fascinating opponent to defeat rather than as a partner. I didn't want to admit that I'd entered the cunning game he'd crafted, forced all those around him into, as though trying to convince me, the Cogs, the Natural Engines, of his genius.

I had accomplished more in a single annual than

Zinc had struggled to accomplish in two decades, and for that, he was bitter.

Another scroll on his desk caught my attention, an intricate drawing of a blend of Wind Walker and Water Shifter features, bark and water braiding in a way that shouldn't have been possible. At the top of the worn scroll were the words *Natural Titans,* and below, the specific sub-beings called *Currents*—a transmutation of beings. One of my first discoveries. I should've learned to stop already.

Unlike with Lufeng, from what Copper had told me of my eldest sister's time at the Palace, the speed of my learning once I'd entered the Palace was not carefully fed and timed. It came as a flood that I couldn't hope to contain. When I first became Zinc's apprentice of alchemy, became immersed, fervent in its pursuit, his trust in me grew, and he believed I had turned my back on my home and people—back then, I truly had. It was as though nothing else mattered except discovery.

I was sure that was both Zinc and Copper's greatest regret with me, offering everything at once, as though they were on their last breaths. Looking back now, this was the two siblings' way of working against one another to get me on their side, as though I were a prize to be won. And Zinc had risen as the haughty victor. At least, at first.

Settled beneath the alchemy instructions for Currents were endless sheets of attempts at extending life, to make Cogs immortal, or something close, like Shifters and Walkers. Most of the sections had been furiously crossed out and scribbled in the margins in Script was the word *unsuccessful* repeatedly. From what Copper had told me, this became his obsession when their parents passed almost two decades ago.

I left it untouched.

How glorious would it be to take away their powers of disaster, so they may never again destroy our homes, never again take any of our lives. Zinc had always believed the Natural Engines, Walkers and Shifters, were to blame for every life taken by waves and storm even though they had no hand in such a thing. I suspected he knew this and simply didn't want to acknowledge the fact. It made the perfect excuse to turn the Palaces from places of worship to gates of divide.

The ashes of the scrolls I'd burnt had scattered from the wind drifting in from the library's glass doors. Perhaps I'd left the door open because I'd wanted to be caught, and perhaps there was a part of me that was disappointed when I wasn't.

With a final glance and an exhaled breath, I made my way to the passage next to the alchemy chamber that would bring me down to the core of Engine, where both Zinc's and my creations awaited death. As I moved an alarm blared, signaling Zinc's imminent return, and for a breath I stilled, waited, before quickly continuing out of the library.

I pulled out my comscreen as it pinged.

At the top, digital notification banners slid down in rapid succession, holding contradictory news from those who rallied behind Zinc, and quieter, those who supported Copper, mainly in Script, though also occasionally in Breath and Song, or a mix of two of them or all three. Thankful for the fluency I'd attained in all the languages, my eyes worked quick to catch every update, swallowing each piece of information like an Engine-dwelling Cog addict swallowing luna rain and luna dust.

The messages I had been waiting for arrived from two different beings.

From Exile Song—*We are on the way.*

From Terracotta Dune—Copper—*The phoenix has managed her escape.*

The phoenix—Lufeng. I took a breath as I reread the message.

From under my white cloak, heat built up within my interior chambers beneath the shell that had replaced my bark. From the ends of the billowing sleeves drifted steam, escaping from the cracked pores of the ashen white-grey of my magma-hardened skin. The plumes thickened as I willed myself to calm, until there were only slivers of vapor quickly dissipating.

I pulled out my mask of dead driftwood, the same

one I wore when I sent Lufeng that first message using my comscreen—a face of bark that would be familiar to my eldest sister, something, *someone,* she could trust. I'd ripped the mask off and discarded it the moment I'd sent the message, the contrast of my hand reminding me that I was a subject of my own alchemy—not just me, but so many others. There was a melancholic sadness, but only for a fleeting moment, at the idea I was no longer the being I once was, the one who was so closely connected to the wind, to Feng. It had been a shedding both willing and unwilling. And it was one I could never take back.

Deception is not natural, is what Grandmother had said, and yet I was a natural at deception—at least that was what Copper told me.

There was one more thing left to do before I was to meet with Exile Song and Lufeng—I had to move quickly before the rebels intercepted her.

The rebels were ready to die for their cause, to die and take Engine down with them by collapsing the iron giant with their corroveins, even if it meant the destruction of their own home in the process. They sought Lufeng as their idol the same way those of the past had sought Grandmother. The Natural Engines and Titans, even the Land Wanderers and Cogs, seemed to believe that a single being can save the world from destruction when it took so much more; they all needed that one being to be the icon of hope through their long, tireless war—or perhaps what they needed was another being to blame if it all failed.

I was certain Grandmother hadn't told Lufeng the truth about her roots, perhaps because she'd regretted telling me. Grandmother's roots were not only connected to Feng, but also to Glace, and to the mountain Engine sat upon, and they were buried so deeply that it was impossible to disconnect the three. If any of the three collapsed, the other two would follow—rotting first at their cores, before decaying altogether. Perhaps she wanted to fall, had always been wishing for it. Was it selfish of me to want her to live, to want to save the homes of many from destruction, even if it meant sacrificing her peace?

All these annuals, she had been so desperately trying to save our home, but we didn't realize she was also trying to save Glace, save Engine—she was also trying to save herself, even though she'd wanted to let go for so long now. But she couldn't. Because of all of us, she continued. Even if all we brought to her in return was pain, sorrow, violence.

I didn't tell Copper that the true reason I'd left the rebels to join her cause was to save my grandmother. Yet, the rebels had believed I had betrayed them, that I wanted to save Engine, and wouldn't listen to any explanation, because their sole desire was to bring Engine down, and the tightly woven system Zinc had built and clung to the strings of like a puppet master.

Yet, if someone were to ask whose side I was on, my true answer would be all and none, because even with the flakes of information I'd collected, it still didn't feel as though I knew enough. I craved more even as all the pieces warred against one another within my mind. But the more I brewed on these supposed truths, the less I was certain about anything. Sometimes, it was worse to make no decision than to make one and be wrong.

4

SANGSHU
THE LAST PUZZLE

The door to the hidden tunnel sat at the back of Zinc's library, the very one that connected the library to another chamber resting behind the water wheel of the Time Teller—a space that once belonged to Copper, now empty. Thinking back, Copper's confinement to the chamber behind the Time Teller, and now shift to the Palace nearest Feng, was evidence of Zinc's efforts to suppress his sister's power over him and Engine. They didn't agree on the direction of Engine's future; Zinc, of course, had no need for anyone who didn't agree with him.

There were several doors throughout the tunnel that hadn't been in use for a while, because Zinc and Copper had, in the past, met at the center of these tunnels for discussions away from prying ears. It was also the place of access to the core of Engine, where Zinc now held captive the failed products of his version of Sun Core alchemy awaiting their fate after he realized what horrific uses they could serve: to be burned to fuel Engine.

From what Copper had told me, this wicked idea of his came shortly after I'd fled, but no one knew what his exact plans were until it was already well in motion. I hadn't found out about the burnings until it was too late—until the chambers at the core had been already built, until the failed Sun Cores had already been trapped within, until too many of them had already lost their lives at the expense of the iron giant and the Iron Alchemist's unwavering cruelty.

Guilt continuously clawed at me from within, during both waking and slumbering moments. It was my discovery, and it felt like it was my fault that this all had happened, even though I couldn't choose what my alchemy was used for. At night, the screams of the failed Sun Cores, mixed with my own, still often echoed in my dreams, an inescapable fever that only broke when I was stirred awake by a barrage of messages and updates from my comscreen. I owed it to them to free them, even if it was at the cost of my own life.

There were three doors on Zinc's half, three on Copper's, opening up to the meeting space in between, with locks requiring specific alchemic patterns only Zinc and Copper would know on each of their respective sides. These couldn't be melted nor broken, but I knew how to open them. Or, at least, had decoded them recently. The first two I was certain about; of the third I was confident, yet a small voice of doubt lingered at the back of my mind.

In front of the first door, I reached out towards the crystal-shaped shard encased in the center. I knew what was necessary for the first two locks—the first puzzle solved by aligning the symbols for the order of silver's alchemy process, the next, gold. Upon the last symbol clicking into place, the puzzle unlocked and allowed access to the second door, where I repeated the process but for gold. Then I halted in front of the third door. Heat grew beneath the surface of my palms, condensation rising and settling at the thought of having only one attempt at the lock and all those who awaited my rescue on the other side. I wiped away the dampness, shook my head of the worry of potential failure—something I hadn't felt in a long time.

I remembered the last time I crossed through these tunnels. I came from Zinc's side to meet Exile Song who came from Copper's. Exile Song was so calm and reassured about his ability to open the door from Copper's end, and I couldn't help but think about the way Copper trusted Exile Song and the way Zinc never truly trusted anyone.

How could a being ever hope for the trust of others if they themselves could not offer the same?

I stared at the last puzzle lock. Before, whenever I

shadowed Zinc to his meetings with Copper, when we reached this last door, he'd always asked me to turn away before he unlocked it. I'd hear the slow clicking before the final symbol slotted into place. At first, I wasn't curious, then, it gradually became almost an obsession. Perhaps that was what Zinc had anticipated; that I'd come to understand him well enough to betray him. Maybe that was why he had stopped with me as his first and last apprentice.

I stared at the door, the lock, then exhaled.

It was so simple and obvious, yet anyone would over-think the answer when considering the complexity of the shape and intricacies of the puzzle. The Palace near Clay seemed as though it were made of sand and stone only, but in fact it had grains of gold mixed within its structure. The Palace near Glace was constructed from layers of stone and silver. It had been a dream of mine to visit, after seeing so many images of it on my comscreen. Exile Song had promised to one day take me. Though now, I wasn't sure if that day would ever arrive.

This left only one Palace—the one made of bone. My fingers were deft as I rearranged the puzzle with the symbols that signified the alchemic processes for the recreation of bone. Zinc would know I'd finally succeeded in opening his lock as soon as he returned because a carcass shifted always left a mark. I welcomed the thought of his discovery, as the tips of my fingers prickled with anticipation.

5

SANGSHU

THE CORE OF ENGINE

On the passage down in the creaking iron leveler that sat at the center of Zinc and Copper's chambers—a platform with a crate-like encasing structure that transported Cogs from one level of Engine to another—I caught glimpses of round metal chambers with the doors shut, a small frosted window at the center, through which shadows shifted across. Each chamber floated, as though suspended in the air, held in place by cylindric pillars at different, staggered heights.

Though I couldn't see through the opaque iron surface of the chambers, I couldn't help but imagine the Cogs who lay unconscious within them—the ones 'testing' their creations, new luxuras made from Moonglow called luna rain and luna dust. Often, the Cogs drank and smoked these into oblivion. And when they woke, hazy-minded, they'd rationalize that their excessive consumption was necessary. "For science," they would say. "For research." This place was not unlike Zinc's library, but instead of experimentation on other beings, the alchemists here would experiment on themselves.

The guards were gone, and it felt too convenient, calculated, but it was difficult trying to decipher Zinc's intentions. I suppressed weariness and pulled out my comscreen. Encrypted messages detailing the movements of those allied with Copper had flooded in over the last few moons.

From Rooted Breath—Aunt Xiangmu—*The wedding has taken place.*

From each of the Puppet Kings—Drought, Flood, Bone—Yunshu, Heshi, Father—*We have distanced ourselves from the phoenix.*

From Terracotta Dune—*Zinc and his guards will return soon.*

I had little time remaining to reach and rescue Blinking Star and the other Sun Cores. It was agonizing to remain patient for the past annual. I couldn't make my move until the rebels made theirs, because only during the chaos of the rebels' operations would Zinc's forces become so divided it would be difficult for him and his guards to stop the Sun Cores from escaping. Lufeng's escape came unexpected, but it served as the perfect, although unintentional, distraction.

At the core of Engine nestled chambers of stone, spherical, with small crevices carved through—enough for oxygen, a finger or two, an eye to peek through. Within each rested a Sun Core. I shuddered at how many of them had already been snatched out of the chambers and pushed into the central hearth, destroyed, burnt, to fuel Engine and its productions. I couldn't help but allow the blame to fester within me for their fate. If I hadn't made this discovery, perhaps none of them would be trapped here now by Zinc. Yet it seemed discovery would always be a double-edged dagger in how it would later be used, and who chose its uses. I couldn't control Zinc's despicable actions, but perhaps I should have foreshadowed the potential consequences. The daunting realization hovered persistently at the back of my mind like scrapping branches at the base of my skull.

From several rows now came a harsh, anxious whisper. "Waiting Sun?"

I hurried towards the sound. They often switched the chambers each Sun Core may inhabit as new additions were funneled in. Sometimes, a chamber held more than one, as though the space within wasn't already restricted enough with the walls closing in on the individual Sun Cores within, who were fruitlessly attempting to make themselves smaller by crouching.

"Blinking Star?" I whispered when I arrived in the general area of her voice, before another low "*here*" drew me towards a stone chamber three spheres down.

I peeked into several crevices. Only darkness greeted me, until—

From one of the small openings near the bottom, a warm breeze wafted through—unnatural, from the alchemy of flesh. The one thing we all had in common: we were all made up of those who had lost their wind affinities. The Natural Engines called those who had undergone the alchemy of flesh Natural Titans, yet what we really had become was fodder—non-renewable and easily disposable. Sun Cores who were incapable of regeneration.

If I asked myself now, why did I do this to myself? Why did I aid Zinc? And why did I allow such a thing to happen to other beings like me? The answer might be one incomprehensible to others. When I became an apprentice to Zinc, I searched constantly for meaning that always seemed to escape me. I was trapped in a body that felt no longer like mine because I had lost my affinity for wind after being in the Palace for so long. My mind had been altered by so many others—by both Copper and Zinc who tried to mold and reshape relentlessly, distorting my dream into one not my own, until it was a reflection of theirs instead.

Watching the Cogs made me realize their anxiety and sorrow, caused by living in a place that was made for them but built on a foundation of the deaths of others. The only way that they could squander their guilt was to forget this fact, pretend it didn't exist, and cling, desperately, to life—even if it meant each breath they took was stolen from others. Copper believed they could live differently, if only shown how, but that took time, and we were running out of it. Regardless of whether I truly trusted her, I had no choice but to follow her, because she wished to save Engine while the rebels wished to fell it, and for Grandmother to survive, Engine must not fall.

I took Blinking Star's chamber lock in my hands, shifted the puzzle the way I had with the third door of Zinc and Copper's connecting chambers—the alchemy for bone—and unlocked her prison. Blinking Star stumbled outwards on quivering legs, steam drifting from every pore of her ashen body, grey and littered with craters and crevices like a battered moon.

The rebels would soon make their move to topple Engine, I was certain. And chaos was the best condition for undetected escape.

"How?" Blinking Star asked, hopeful yet weary.

I took her hand in mine—hers burning from being in the flames of the chamber and mine cold from inhibiting the heat of the inferno tears within me, my shell like the surface of a dormant volcano—and showed her the puzzle for the locks. She stared down at our joined hands, eyes wide. Her fingers tightened around mine, as though she were afraid of letting go. I squeezed back in return.

Blinking Star refocused on the motion of my other

hand as I repeated the pattern of the puzzle for the chamber locks once more on the back of her hand. Blinking Star took a sharp breath; at the same moment an almost familiar scream echoed in the distance like a howl down a mountain, seeming to rattle the metallic walls of each sitting chamber. Still hand in hand, both of us flinched at the sound. Instead of letting go, we clutched on tighter, even though our expressions remained neutral.

We held our breaths to the sound of sizzling water evaporating into steam, and my mind was haunted by the image of Water Shifters jumping to their deaths to cool down Engine machinery.

Then another scream came, one that Blinking Star and I knew well—the sound of a Sun Core being thrown into the hearth, eyes still open. That could have been her. That could have been me.

If these Natural Engines cannot shift water nor borrow wind, what is the use of them? Your sacrifices are so important. They make up the foundation of all we have created and continue to create. Isn't that what gods are for? Natural gods? Natural Engines to serve those who have no such powers themselves? Zinc had said this, as though we are at fault for the fragility of Cogs.

How many of the lives here had cycled through death and life, almost death and almost life at the mercy of my alchemy? Even if indirectly.

A soft sob escaped Blinking Star. Her head shook.

She had a face of shattered, dusted features like the lightless side of a cratered moon.

The desolate tone to her voice brewed anger within me.

Dying was a key part of becoming a Sun Core, but it wasn't as simple as that, and I was reminded again of Zinc's failure in the form of all the Sun Cores trapped within the chambers. They were not full Sun Cores because the one thing necessary for the complete alchemy of flesh to become a Sun Core was not a physical transmutation but an internal transformation: the willingness to die—not one as a result of defeat, the loss of will to live, but an intentional sacrifice, to stare down a path without knowing the destination and have the courage to take the step.

To let go of time, the concept of life and death, to see oneself as a part of a cycle rather than being apart from it, as something *more*. This acceptance was an almost impossible, morbid ask.

Zinc had always perfected the chemical but never had he the psychological—the one thing that held him back from the full potential greatness of a master alchemist.

I pulled a comscreen from my robes and pressed it into Blinking Star's hands. "Free the others and wait for my message. Stay hidden. Close the chamber doors behind you to make it seem as though you are all still inside."

Blinking Star nodded, then offered a reassuring gaze that seemed to say, *Don't worry about me.*

But how could I not? I had created them. The Currents, the Orics, the Sun Cores—the Natural Titans. The Currents were an unintended discovery in aiding Zinc's research for Cog immortality; the Orics as a counter to Currents who'd become rebels and caused the corroveins. The first Sun Cores I'd alchemized in order to save withering Wind Walkers who had given up on living, because they'd lost their affinities for wind or water, and wanted to feel connected once more, to something, anything, even if it meant that thing would be fire and flames. Yet as a consequence, those who came after had become fodder for Cog survival. Creation after creation aimed to serve as a solution but created instead an unending spiral of unintended consequences.

I squandered the rising anger within me, smothered it so that it became nothing but a dull, numb throbbing instead. If I allowed the answer to fester, the inferno tears within me to flow, I wouldn't be able to control who I may accidentally hurt. Exile Song's evaporated arm came to mind. I wouldn't allow such a thing to happen again.

From behind one of the stone chambers, a Cog scurried. It was Nickel—a friend of Copper's late daughter Brass, a comrade of mine now, who had succumbed to an incurable fever caused by the rising internal temperature of Engine. I believe that was what spurred Copper, finally, towards change, towards the desire to overthrow Zinc—when a loved one was ripped from her hands, and the fault rested with her ancestors and her brother.

"I'll make sure she's safe," Nickel whispered, taking a step close to Blinking Star, seemingly unconcerned by the smoke wafting from her body.

I nodded. "Thank you."

Trust was something easy to shatter and gruelingly difficult to build. Yet, seeing Blinking Star and Nickel standing side by side, I had hope it was possible. These were two individuals who were somehow able to trust one another, even given Zinc's efforts to keep Natural Engines and Titans, and the Cogs separate, disconnected—Zinc's conviction that Natural Engines and Titans were only meant to be seen as tools had been adopted by so many Cogs over time. In my stead, Nickel had visited the chambers, Blinking Star and the others, disrupted the heat settings, turned them off when they could. Whether it was out of guilt, empathy, or something else, their action no doubt moved Blinking Star, as it had moved me and convinced me of what Copper had been advocating for—that Cogs and Natural Engines and Titans could coexist peacefully. That Engines and Titans need not continue to die. That Grandmother could continue to stand rather than fall.

Once, I'd asked Brass what changed her mind, about the Engines and Titans, and if it was because of her mother's, Copper's, own beliefs, even though she never seemed to push them upon her own daughter. Brass told me that when she turned off her comscreen, stopped listening to all the other voices telling her what and how she should be thinking—the loudest of which was Zinc's endless droning—she found a greater clarity, and with it recognized the impending self-destruction of Engine and the Cogs if things were to remain the same. I was certain this was the same for Nickel.

As I left Blinking Star, I thought of her true name, Euca, and of how she had spoken it in a low whisper, more directed to herself than me, right before I'd alchemized her. She told me she regretted leaving Feng and asked if I regretted doing the same, even knowing our circumstances were different—that I didn't have a choice. Just like with Brass, who had also asked me if I regretted leaving Feng, I couldn't give Blinking Star the answer she sought because I didn't regret it.

I was glad I'd left.

If I hadn't, I would not have discovered all that I knew now, regardless of whether it was beneficial or detrimental.

I'd told Blinking Star she would be okay, that she could trust me, in selfishness, because I had been so confident, too much so, in my alchemy, because I hadn't realized what Zinc had planned for the Sun Cores. I'd only desired to offer a different affinity in the place of the one they'd lost.

I took the leveler down to the base of Engine before leaving through an escape route chewed through the base of its foundations by the corroveins—I supposed I should thank the rebels for the unintentional aid.

Outside of Engine, by the base of the iron giant's body, I stared up at the library's opened doors amid the backdrop of the clouds that always hid the sun beneath. Leading up to the library were layers upon layers of individual chambers, some topped with slanted, flat-tiled roofs while others ended in the sharp points of turrets. The iron giant rested on top of a flattened mountain peak. The sections of Engine's base glowed a dim amber where rust crawled upwards towards the library, corroveins pulsing, flaking like dead skin.

The sight of Engine's rot festering reminded me of Grandmother. I had always thought Grandmother put on a brave front, yet when I crossed over to the other side of the wall, I realized she had never truly hidden her vulnerabilities, not like Zinc. She always had presented them plain, much like her unhidden roots that grew above rather than below ground, into the skies that made up our homes. If we had looked close enough, which none of us had, we would've noticed the decay, the growing rot, of someone ancient and ready to pass on, yet expected to be immortal because none of us knew how to survive without her. Such a weight shouldn't have rested upon a single tree with weakened roots. What we should've done was strengthen our own roots rather than always taking shelter within hers until she could no longer hold us up. Perhaps that was what she'd always hoped for—us to notice—except none of us ever did, because we were too busy staring within ourselves, aimlessly.

6

LUFENG
THE SEA BELOW

Just as my eyes were about to close, mind drifting from exhaustion, Chuiliu jarred me from my near slumber.

"Fengfeng," she whispered, urgent, nudging me from the side.

The island of Gear grew closer. I spotted a cloaked figure with their hood up, waiting by the sandy shores. The running sap within me quickened at the thought of seeing Sangshu again. Exile Song's gaze held a strange intensity as his stare fixated in the same direction. But, before I could take a closer look at the figure's face beneath the drawn hood of the cloak, confirming whether it was indeed my fourth sister, fog shrouded the rest of the world from view in every direction, like storm tree leaves clustering together.

I drew into my arms Chuiliu and Changqing, who were nesting within the Traveler's cradle as the fog thickened, until I could barely see the top of Chuiliu's needle threads even though she sat against me. My fingers tightened around the shoulders of my siblings, and I winced at the thought that perhaps my grip, digging into their bark, was hurting them, but I would regret it more if I were to be separated from them again like I had been back at the Palace.

"Geyser— Exile Song—" the names choked in my throat as several hands, with flesh of churning currents belonging to Shifters, clawed up the sides of the Traveler. My mind was on high alert, eyes darting around for potential escape, for safety, neither of which existed as we remained stranded on the Traveler in the middle of deep waters.

"No!" Exile Song shouted, lurching forward—too late. My breath caught in my throat when I felt my siblings being tugged in different directions.

With a yelp, Changqing was ripped from my grasp, and his small body tumbled over the edge of the Traveler, disappearing into the sea below. Then Chuiliu was pulled over on my other side, her voice muffled by the water crashing against metal. My fingers met thin air as they clutched, desperately, futilely, in the directions my siblings had disappeared in—thrashing against the surface of the unstill waters, causing ripples to scatter outwards before they were quickly lost, swallowed by the endless waves.

My straggled voice tore from me in a hoarse gurgle, the same moment Exile Song shouted my name, as I was dragged backwards by my cloak. My hands flung out, reaching for him to no avail. My mind had surrendered before my body, my feet thrashing as I tumbled over the side of the Traveler in a mess of flailing limbs.

There was no time to tighten my pores before the back of my head broke the surface of the sea, my mouth agape, overflowing with water. My bark stiffened at the impact as the invader pulled me deeper and deeper into the water's depths. Piercing streams flooded into each gasping pore, threatening to drown me.

7

SANGSHU

WHERE WATER RISES

From the shore of Gear, I blinked at the Traveler floating forth, then squinted because a thick veil of fog blew across the machine and its passengers. As quickly as the Traveler disappeared, it re-emerged several moments later. As the Traveler grew closer to Gear's shoreline, leaving its surrounding shroud behind, it was clear Exile Song was alone.

The plan was to have Lufeng and Exile Song escape together. Confusion raised the temperature at my temples to an almost uncomfortable heat. With a breath, I calmed myself until smoke no longer swirled and wafted outwards from the white tendrils that were my hair, now hidden in the shadows of my cloak. That was the aspect of my changed appearance that would be most difficult to hide from Lufeng. There would be no need now.

Where was she?

My rough fingers tightened around my dead driftwood mask and gloves as I ripped them off, allowing my arms to sit exposed by throwing back the long billowing sleeves of the tattered old Feng cloak I had traded my white one for. I almost laughed at the irony, of me criticizing Zinc and Copper's strategic cunning when in fact I was behaving just like them. *Many trust those who resemble them—it's a natural instinct,* was what Zinc told me as he debated between two cloaks before deciding he'd wear both: a blue one in the morning, a green one during the evening. With the extravagant way Zinc presented himself, it was almost as though he was saying, *Regardless of my appearance, I can gain trust in seconds and crush the same with the same brevity.*

I thought bitterly of the way that even those sharing the same blood, sap, or current running, dripping or pulsing within them might turn on one another, might become so different in their values and beliefs, past the point of reconciliation. I think of the ally I thought I'd found in Zinc, the new and still shaky trust with Copper.

As the Traveler floated towards me, I watched the surrounding waters, dark and unsteady, for potential ambush. Though the waves were loud, all else seemed far too quiet. Zinc and his guards, I knew, would not give chase. He had something else planned. I was sure.

There had been news through my comscreen of a rally he was to hold shortly on Engine. He would already be on his way back to the iron giant, if he wasn't already there.

As the Traveler docked against the shore, I pulled on one of my gloves again and reached out a hand to help Exile Song out of the machine. Guilt chewed from within at the sight of Exile Song's missing arm beneath the limp flutter of the sleeve of his robe.

As Exile Song climbed out, the Traveler pushed away from the shore, adrift once more, passengerless. Though he tried to balance himself once he let go of my hand, Exile Song seemed unsteady. The currents running beneath his translucent skin rippled, the flow periodically disturbed by an unseen force. Horrified, I realized he had been alchemized with far more oric than I'd left creation instructions for. The plan had been for him to smuggle out the very alchemized substance that could counter the rust of corroveins, could scrub the iron clean of it—not to infuse himself with it! I thought again of the Water Shifters who sacrificed their lives to cool down Engine, and I suppressed the thought that Exile Song might have planned to do the same to get rid of the corroveins.

For a moment, I wanted to shout at him, to reprimand him for the risk he had taken. I allowed my temper to simmer, and the single glove on my hand turned to ashes in seconds. Exile Song reached out, then allowed his hand to drop, and I knew both of us thought back to when I had been first alchemized. I didn't blame him, only myself.

Heat prickled the surface of my shell. We'd have to find an opportunity to extract the oric before it destabilized him further and before the substance became too infused. It felt as though I'd already lost so much, to Zinc, to Engine, and I didn't want to lose any more, and yet, I knew I would, for Grandmother, for all our homes.

Exile Song nodded, briefly, once, a hint of forlorn desolation in his expression.

"Are you alright?" I whispered. For a moment, on impulse, he was the one now to reach forward before allowing his slightly raised arm to fall back to his side again.

"Yes," he murmured in Song. To any unfamiliar with the language, it might have only sounded like a muffled burble from a river stream lost to the vastness of the surrounding dominant sea. To me, it sounded like the familiar, gentle rising and falling of waves near seashores.

"Where is she," I asked quietly in Song. A statement, not a question.

I was told by Grandmother that Lufeng was the only one grown directly from her roots and the one who would be used as her stand-in at the Iron Alchemist's rally. I knew Zinc had originally wanted Lufeng to show the Cogs that he had conquered the Natural Engines. He desired to show all of Engine, and the Natural Engines and Titans trapped on Gear, that even gods were not invincible.

I'd asked, *Why go through the trouble when you could use any other Wind Walker or Water Shifter, and the Cogs wouldn't ever know the difference?*

Zinc had tutted, shaken his head in disappointment, as he said, *But* I *would.* Then, with a sigh, he murmured, *No one can say I never work hard for what I wish to possess and accomplish.*

Zinc kept us distant and unseen for a reason. Natural Titans like me warranted even closer watch, at least from the rest of Engine and the Cogs.

Exile Song shook his head. "The rebels." He looked away. "They have Chuiliu and Changqing as well."

Our siblings. My finger curled into fists, and though I knew the rebels meant no harm to Lufeng nor our siblings, it was obvious they would use the saplings to convince her of their cause.

At this moment, the rebels seemed no different from Zinc, willing to manipulate, to destroy, to achieve their goals, or in this case, for vengeance, for freedom, even if it meant further collapse. Justifying, at this very moment, within their minds, the necessity of the manipulation. I almost laughed at the irony.

"Why were the little ones with you?" I asked. "That was not the plan."

"I—" Exile Song couldn't meet my eyes.

I exhaled slowly. It was likely Lufeng's decision. One I should have predicted. It seemed I had fallen victim to carelessness of thought, considering only the short-term rather than long-term consequences and variations in results.

I stared at the sea as though it would offer me an explanation. With eyes closed, I focused on the sounds behind me—the iron-bladed wings, clicking like talons on branches as they sliced clean swoops through the wind, churned by the Walker-produced gusts, and the crash of waves tumbling from water wheels from the efforts of Shifters. Both the breezes and flow of water were stronger today—someone must have been thinking about their home, someone must have been missing their past. Within me, the ache that should've been present at the thought was nothing but a dull, warm throb.

I thought about how on some days it was windless and waveless, though those days were rare now, and whenever the calm arrived, it made me anxious rather than settled. It had been a long time since I felt settled.

The rebels would use Lufeng as a shield. Against me.

I was once one of those rebels, for a time so brief I wasn't sure if I could truly say I was ever a part of them. I couldn't remain. Those Natural Engines and Titans were no better than Zinc, wishing for the destruction of Engine as though more death was the unrivalled solution. *If they will not listen, then we will make it so they won't have to.*

My reply was left to silence—*So your solution is to become just like them?*

Copper thought it was possible to find a middle ground for Engine to remain standing without the deaths of Natural Engines and Titans, if Zinc were displaced from his role of authority. Even outside of my own motives of saving Grandmother so Feng and Glace might remain standing, even if it meant Engine would too, I had come to believe that there were those living within the iron giant who we could trust, who we could work with rather than be used by, like Nickel. The Cog had told me that it was possible for them to adapt, over time, with help—a collaboration between the Natural Engines and the Cogs rather than mutual destruction. Yet, Zinc didn't want to accept any solution that he himself hadn't come up with.

If Grandmother could see me at this moment. I remembered once I said to her, *You have such a gentle heart filled with mercy for even the cruelest of death bringers.*

And her response, *If I do not, then who will?*

Exile Song and I looked to one another, and he offered a subtle nod. We knew we couldn't remain here.

Engine loomed in the distance, and soon, it would fall because the rebels would no doubt act swiftly with Lufeng's presence spurring them forth and inspiring in them confidence. We had to mobilize all of Copper's allies in preparation for a counter, to confront the rebels at the iron giant.

"It will take us a while to travel across Gear unnoticed," I muttered, wincing at the reminder that I could no longer borrow wind. The inferno within me quivered, an unseen reaction pushing against the interior of my creviced shell—discomfort and unease at something that used to calm me, that used to feel familiar, *natural.*

On Gear, the Shifters and Walkers almost never left their posts, forced to borrow wind and shift water to power the Churners and Wheels that kept Engine going. I bowed my head at the reality of what Zinc had created, something I had once overlooked because of my curiosity for alchemy. It was also a guilt I had to overcome.

"Sangshu—" Exile Song turned to me with his sleeve raised, the other fluttered, empty, like a wing ready for flight. I flinched at my true name. True names of both Natural Engines and Natural Titans were almost never used in Engine. "Waiting Sun," he quickly corrected himself.

"We need to go," was all I said before I turned and hurried towards the outer edges of Gear's surrounding shores and the remaining trees scattered near the waters. I wanted to linger in this reunion but knew we couldn't spare the time.

Behind a cluster rested a refashioned Traveler that had been infected by corroveins. Its bird legs sat at half the height, because I had to trim the already collapsing infected half, decreasing its stride length, and its recalibrated system meant a slower speed as well. It would take almost twice as long to reach the Eternal Bridges compared to a traditional Traveler, but it would have to do. It had been impossible to steal a functioning Traveler from Zinc and his guards because of the newest identification system they'd implemented, and the one Exile Song had escaped in was far beyond repair.

I hopped into the reworked Traveler. Exile Song was ginger in his climb after me.

He settled behind me, leaning heavily against the back of the machine, arm resting on his legs, head dipped forth, hanging, almost brushing against my back. For a moment, I wished for him to fall forward, to lean on me the way I'd always leaned on him in the past. The thought of our promised visit to Glace loomed once more—a dream so seemingly faraway now. I shook the thought from my mind and turned my attention to the control panel, which was scratched but useable. I tapped the start button, propelling the contraption forward in its creaking walk. I kept my hand hovering over the controls with its various flat symbols for further direction maneuver.

The rebels would soon make for Engine and

await their moment to strike during or after Zinc's rally. Those loyal to Copper would need to prepare to counter. I sent a message to Copper through my comscreen, though I knew it was likely she would have already caught wind of the progression. Her response was instantaneous.

I will evacuate the Palace before regrouping with you, Exile Song, and Elder Yinxing in the case of our confrontation with the rebels spiraling outwards, away from Engine. Which may be likely.

I replied with an affirmation and returned my attention to the path ahead.

As we made for the Eternal Bridges, the crunch of the Traveler's legs in the sand sounded like serrated bone against bark. I trained my eyes forward and willed them not to look back at the Churners and Wheels as we rounded the outer edge of Gear, our path the curve of a scythe left in the terracotta earth.

8

LUFENG
EYES AND MOUTHS

When I woke, sputtering from my pores, disorientation sprung me towards action as I scrambled upwards, uprooting dry soil and scant grass beneath me. A scatter of trees surrounded me, some grouped, though the density of the clusters were far from the lush immensities of Feng—almost as though wind had sporadically whisked up trees and placed them elsewhere, away from sight.

Chuiliu and Changqing were nowhere to be found, and neither were our potential takers. Exile Song, too, was gone, and I recalled his shocked expression being the last thing I saw as I fell, no, was *pulled* into the water. Perhaps he was already on his way. Perhaps he had already found Chuiliu and Changqing. Sap ran hot within me, my pulse thudding at my throat.

Frantic, I scanned the surrounding area for possible clues for where I was and where my siblings were, pacing towards and away, unsure in which direction I should first search.

Several steps away were some things I had once seen in the books at the Palace library—tracks for transportation, snaking all the way through this floating land, extending outwards over the sea towards Engine. Along the tracks were a steady stream of iron crates, evenly spaced, gliding forth. Then, I spotted the unnatural, crawling corroveins, trailing like the veins of Land Wanderers waiting to burst from their flesh—dark, damp, earthen in color.

Then, the sound of wind and water drew my attention to iron towers, bladed, slicing through the sky in an endless cycle, wheels of water churning without pause, peeking through the branches of reaching trees. In the stream, I blinked, then squinted when I noticed there was the occasional opening of an eye, a break, an interruption. I was sure I saw wrong, until I saw another, and another, and another, and—

I clutched at myself, bracing, when I realized there were not only eyes but also mouths that held no words, they opened but came not sounds. The constant fall of water with these faceless eyes and mouths vicious, unyielding, heartbreaking. My bark tightened at the sight, stilling me in place until I realized it might be dangerous to remain so vulnerable and visible.

I crawled forth, legs still too weak from almost drowning. From the brush I was hidden beneath, my far-reaching sight allowed me to spot the Wind Walkers commanding breeze to drive forth the spinning iron blades, and Water Shifters guiding the cycle of water over the wheels. All of them wore solemn, withered expressions, with an almost mechanical tiredness to the way they moved their limbs, as though wanting to stop but not being able to, going through the movements aimlessly. I had never seen anyone so dispirited, not since Mother. I swallowed the bitter thought of Mother still trapped in the Palace, now alone, and hoped Father was able to keep her safe after my escape.

I raised my hands, reaching towards the towers and wheels, wanting nothing more than to close the eyes of those stuck in the endless cycle, to stop the silent screams, to pull the Wind Walkers and Water Shifters away from the towers and blades and wheels and the dead water, when a voice halted me.

"Don't."

My hands withdrew, and I turned, upper body only, legs still weak and barely mobile.

An unfamiliar being emerged first from behind a tree. Behind them gathered Wind Walkers and Water Shifters I did not recognize, and among them were those that were a blend of Walker and Shifter. *Currents* was what Exile Song had called them. The sight of them caused me to shudder, reminding me of the experimental chambers I had found in the Palace.

"What...?" I glanced back towards the iron towers with blades and the wheels.

"Churners and Wheels used to power Engine," the Current standing in front of the group said, voice quiet, low. He continued in bitter murmur, "Fallen gods, fallen engines, that's what they call us."

In the distance, past the Churners, Wheels, the bridges, sat the giant iron entity I had only seen from afar, from within the confines of the Palace. Here, it seemed far too close, as though a single gust of wind would deliver me to its gates.

"And all... this?" I gestured towards the tracks, the crates.

The Current walked forth, knocked on a crate moving by. "From Clay, sorted through the Palace, delivered across Gear before making its way to Engine."

He pried one iron covering open, keeping in stride with the steady forward movement of it. A Wind Walker lifted me into the air so we could follow behind. Though my body was still weighed down by water, I hadn't felt so light in a while.

When the wind brought me close enough, I saw what lay inside the crate. Plants and creatures—birds of various kinds, deer like the one we had at the ceremony, fish and other life found at sea—fresh, so much so I could have almost believed they were still alive. But then, there were other crates, opened, exposed, of plants with their roots severed, creatures with cuts and wounds on their gutted bodies that looked clean, but their violence was glaring.

The Current opened another crate heading in the opposite direction, back towards the Palace, the other side of the wall—waste, excess, further carcasses laying unburied, uprooted plants rotten and unconsumed, mold festering. I thought back to the ceremony, how not all the food had been consumed, whisked away by the Taskers, discarded somewhere unseen. There were lives that need not have been taken.

I looked away, unable to stand the sight further, because it evoked in me both the familiar sensation of a stomach-churning disgust but also the salivating allure of that first taste of meat. I resisted the urge to spit, to scrape clean my throat of that taste I could no longer forget, the very one I sometimes found myself unconsciously craving to my own horror.

My attentions snapped to the Walker who had lifted me as they guided water from a nearby stream, had it hovering by me, as if waiting for me to drink. Nearby, a Shifter, previously hidden in the crowd, walked forward. Settled upon their shoulder was a small unfamiliar sapling.

The sapling reminded me of Chuiliu. Of Changqing.

"Where—" I began, eyes scrambling to scan the group around me for their faces as I whirled in a circle, drawing around me thin drifts of wind, barely strong enough to carry upwards the leaves scattered on the ground beneath the surrounding trees.

"Your siblings are safe. Don't worry."

A fury rose within me at the calmness of this stranger's words, and I attempted to propel myself forward on instinct, only to be halted by a strong gust of wind from the nearby Walker with the sapling. I stumbled until I fell backward, nails digging into the hard clumped and crumbled soil.

"Your father and mother too. We can save them." The Current stepped forward, reached out a hand towards me. For a moment I reached out, then let my hand drop. I pushed myself from the ground alone and took several steps backward.

This was familiar.

I will help you if—

If you don't help me then—

What was the difference between Zinc's threatening and this Current's bargain? There always seemed to be a condition. Help was never given out willingly. A frustrated lump built in my throat like a dam in the middle of a stream. I attempted to borrow wind, willed it to gather around my hands, but my fingers quivered, still too weak. It would be impossible to overpower anyone here in my current state— or even if I were rested. It seemed the beings here were versed in borrowing wind not only for travels but manipulating it for other purposes; perhaps even combat from the way some of them stood, eyes scanning the area, as though predators waiting to strike. They were so different from the calm nature of the Wind Walkers back in Feng.

"Please listen to what I have to say, first, and I will take you to your siblings," the Current said, holding up two palms.

I felt the Current's stare trained on me as I gazed at the iron giant ahead.

"I am listening," I said—even though that was the last thing I desired—without looking back in the Current's direction.

"We plan to destroy Engine," the Current said, then I could hear the slow smile leaking into his next words. "Is this not what you, too, want?"

It was clear he already knew the answer I would give yet waited in patience for me to reveal it anyhow. These must be the rebels that Exile Song had spoken about. The ones responsible for the corroveins. The Current's words lingered within me, and I could not help but feel as though they were withholding information from me. Much like how everyone back at the Palace had.

The Wind Walker carried me forth once more using wind, and I allowed them without resistance, knowing it was better to conserve my energy. I looked to the Current as we grew closer to the bridges, where the crates, too, headed towards the iron giant. I knew now why these Churners and Wheels were placed on a separate floating land, far from where the 'Cogs' could see, why we the 'Natural Engines'—at least those who refused to comply—were left on the other side of the wall, slowly destroyed out of sight. Because if they saw us, truly knew us, they might feel guilt, regret. But hidden away, we were nothing but a means to an end.

Finally, I turned to the Current. I shut my eyes, and after another long moment of silence, I said, "Yes."

"What do I call you?" I then asked. Mother had once said, *Never trust a being who does not give you their true name.* And yet, Zinc seemed to prove the opposite could also be true.

"You can simply call me… Fog."

9

SANGSHU

WHERE WIND FALLS

To become the final victor, you must fight not the obvious battles but the ones unseen, the ones your opponents allow to slip through the cracks, so by the time they notice, the culmination of your smaller wins and feigned losses will result in your ultimate triumph. Aunt Xiangmu told me this after my 'marriage' negotiations.

The contracts, a war of quiet politics, but movement behind the scenes was what would create the shifts—a slow revolution that had been brewing amid the unraveling seams of the push and pull of Zinc and Copper's false united front.

Exile Song shifted from his sitting position within the Traveler so that he was now standing, his shadow looming over me. From this side of Gear closer to the Palaces, I could spot corroveins on Engine, crawling like pulsing vines, growing ever more rampant along the large iron body, stuttering the once-smooth turning of the water wheel that drew from the surrounding sea and poured like a waterfall from the top of the metal giant.

The Eternal Bridges stretched like straight-edged rivers of slate between Gear and Engine, trekking across the dark sea—three different belts endlessly moving forward in a steady rhythm both above and below in two different directions, running through the island of Gear, wrapping around the two ends of an otherwise unbending body. Magnetized iron crates travelled in uniformed distances along each of the bridges. Below, occasional Treaders sailed across the wide canals between each bridge, carrying Land Wanderer merchants towards Engine with their rarest wares for wealthy Cogs. Though no matter how much the Cogs begged nor bribed, they themselves never passaged from Engine towards Gear, much less the other side of the wall.

We want to see the gods too—the Natural Engines we've heard so much about.

No, they're too dangerous. We've only gotten some of them under control.

Keeping them out of the public's eye was Zinc's way of controlling the Cogs' opinions about the Natural Engines—the less they knew and understood, the better.

When we reached the mouth of the central bridge, I set a command for the Traveler to settle itself among the rocks near where the sea poured down in a waterfall into a continued vastness, before Exile and I hopped off. From here, it seemed as though Engine nested atop a mountain raised from the waters below, just to serve as its sturdy foundation.

I tossed Exile Song a friction slider that would magnetize itself to the side of the bridge and bring us across to Engine—slower than the wind, yet safer than the water, and faster than traveling with the crates on the belt itself. Exile Song weighed the slider in his hand: the slender silver bar seemed much smaller curled in his fingers as he adjusted his grip around the rubberized, cylindrical handle at the center of two protruding points which looked like the occasional turrets atop Engine that partially made up its roofing.

Both of us snapped on bangles of the same material as the slider to help with stability before crouching down to secure the sliders onto the side of the platform, the thick, immobile strip on which the belts roamed across. This was the fastest way to travel for beings who had lost their affinities to wind and water. It wasn't allowed. But it didn't matter.

Exile Song stepped off the ledge. At first, he seemed rusty in his movement, but he quickly adapted, becoming relaxed in his posture and evident in the loose yet firm grip of his single hand. His easy confidence was something I missed, as well as his awareness, which I was reminded of when he turned to look at me with a tilt of his head, as though he knew I was staring. I allowed myself a small smile, then nodded. I felt the small space between the platform and slider vibrate before allowing myself to step off the ledge after Exile Song.

Airborne, our bodies dangled far above the sea below, our cloaks collecting moisture drifting from the rush of water now behind us. Mist wafted upwards, sizzling when it met my exposed face. It was exhilarating, every time I used the slider, because of how similar it was to traveling by wind. Yet, it was also melancholic because I knew the feeling was a pale comparison at best.

Occasionally, an onyx watcher drifted past, accompanying a Sea Treader in the waters below. Zinc's obsession with surveillance, of ensuring there were devices that served as his eyes littered across all of Engine, had only gotten worse over the annuals. My nose wrinkled at the sudden metallic scent mixed with a must of rot and rust. I realized it came from an upcoming section of the bridge which festered with corroveins I could spot past Exile's head and hanging arm, hand gripped comfortably around the slider above.

Luckily, the activity on the bridge was not monitored too closely. The onyx watchers were much easier to bypass with the cover of the iron crates—the transported goods were one of their primary concerns. From what I understood, the watchers were also mostly present to observe the recent overheating issues and growing veins, in case any of the crates required maintenance or if a part of the bridge had become so rust-eaten that it required complete replacement. Its metallic scent was almost the twin of the old and dried blood of Cogs, as well as in its coppery hue.

More and more of the iron crates fell victim to the corroveins as well.

Do you know why rust is so harmful? It makes things brittle. Engine, the wheels, the turbines—but the metal creations themselves aren't the only ones growing rust, isn't that right? Zinc had whispered this more to himself than to me under candlelight one night while he was waiting for the results of his latest alchemy experiment—infusing a willing Cog with what he believed was the correct formula to transform them into a Wind Walker. The Cog died in the chamber, and Zinc couldn't bring himself to enter it for the following week. But those periods of mourning drastically decreased with each death that met and left his hands until he only stared, glassy eyed, at the lifeless bodies he asked guards in a monotoned murmur to remove from the library and discard.

In front of me on the belt, Exile Song flinched. It had been a while since Exile Song's last ride, and the possibility of the drop could quiver even the strongest of minds and bodies. But then Exile Song turned his head back with a melancholic yet slightly excited smile on his face, reminding me that he hailed from Glace, and that diving from the top of immense waterfalls, *becoming* a part of that same plummeting water, was what made him feel most alive. I smiled, almost tranquil in the moment, as the two of us were propelled forward on the belt with the crates.

Again, I was reminded of Exile Song's promise to take me to Glace, when he told me of his true name, back when I thought trust was impossible and he'd shown me that it wasn't. He became the one unwavering presence within my life—truly ironic, with the ever-shifting nature of Water Shifters.

The pace of the crates was steady, slow, to create the illusion of scarcity, to make certain goods even more desirable—a contradiction of what Engine stood for: convenience, efficiency, and more recently, excess. Where Cogs constantly chased after the newest creation, the Iron Alchemist fed them promises of what was to come without considering the consequences of rapid, destabilizing production. This was the opposite of what Copper wished for—a slow and stable progress that could help mitigate consequences and the ravaging force of materialism and endless craving.

At first, the advancements were more to busy idle hands and minds and curious budding alchemists like Zinc when he was younger, but then it evolved to become more about control, laying claim to discovery, a pushing of limits and possibilities, of evolutions and revolutions that created solution for solution for solution, reinventing the same things again and again but in doing so creating further problems instead—and hiding them. The Cogs didn't see what occurred on Gear, what was happening behind the walls they called protection and conservation, or perhaps some of them did and chose to look the other way. In becoming Zinc's apprentice, I had fallen into the same cadence—with discovery, with pretending I couldn't see its potential consequences, with the Sun Cores and other Titans, with what it meant for Engine, for the mountain it stood upon, for Grandmother, who was barely holding everything together.

We neared a section of the bridge that was particularly infested with veins, causing the belt to sputter and halt every few exhales until we reached it, and then it stopped altogether as though encountering an abrupt, invisible wall. I swung in place, like a pendulum, legs dangling beneath me, causing brief moments of prickling to rise and linger beneath my hardened skin, jutting needles seeking escape. My breaths stuttered each time the slider halted for seconds at a time as it moved over the decaying pieces of the belt.

Then, there was a strangled shout, and a side of Exile Song's slider slipped from where it held onto the bridge. My grip tightened around my own slider as I willed myself to calm instead of throwing my arm outwards in Exile Song's direction. I would only unsteady myself further. Steam escaped through my pores, billowing around me, as I attempted to slow my panicked breathing. I caught sight of the flakes of rust that had accumulated on the bridge belt's surface, weakening the slider's magnetic hold.

I glanced up at my own slider and noticed the same. My eyes widened as I glanced behind, noticing how long of a stretch remained between us and Engine. The belt creaked, inched slightly forward, swinging me far too close to the vein infestation. I swung my body with my legs split, side to side, oscillating but careful that I didn't accidentally knock into Exile Song, hoping that I could propel myself sideways onto the belt, to try to catch hold of the edge with my hands before my slider's grip gave away.

Then Exile Song's slider detached from the bridge entirely while I was attempting my swing, and he was sent plunging downwards. My mouth fell open in a horrified gasp the same moment my hand caught hold of the edge of the belt. I kicked my legs in his direction, frantic, almost catching his head with my foot in the process. Exile Song threw his arm outwards towards me, caught hold first of my cloak, choking me for a breath before he let go. I flung my hand out on impulse even knowing there was no way to catch hold of him now.

"No!" My words turned to a shout of surprise when Exile Song grabbed my ankle instead. We were only a couple of seconds from falling. Now, a different panic filled me as I tried to grab hold of the edge of the belt with both hands, the scrap of the hard shell of my skin making an uncomfortable grainy sound as I worked to maintain my position. I gritted my teeth, the grinding of bone louder in my mind than the waves below.

"Hold—"

My slider quivered, losing its grip on the bridge, before releasing its hold altogether. At the same time, my hands slipped off the edge of the belt, leaving Exile Song and I to plummet towards the sea below. Flakes of rust followed us down from above like terracotta snow. Suddenly, my mind filled with the image of my body hardening, drowning, if I met water, became entirely submerged. I held my breath. Squeezed my eyes shut. Prepared myself for impact. I could still feel Exile Song's grip around my hand, tight, as though trying to comfort me rather than clinging onto an impossible lifeline.

I knew not how to swim. The sizzling of the exposed parts of my outer shell caused me to hiss while Exile

Song simply shuddered. Though the water would not normally be a danger to Exile Song, at the moment, he was more of a hazard *to* the water now than the water was to him. For me, it was a different matter—I could harden, the tears of the sun within me cool and evaporate and turn me to stone.

I imagined myself sinking, frozen, until I reached the bottom of the sea, at a depth where no one could find me, and no one would care to. I could feel the simmering heat within me waiting to be smothered as both Exile Song and I continued our descent, our cloaks billowing as helplessly as our tensed bodies, doing nothing to slow our fall.

But instead of meeting the sea, the harsh collision, I suddenly felt an opposing pressure from beneath. I glanced towards Exile Song and saw he was somehow paused in the air in a bobbing hover. First came shock that sent a shiver through me, then came relief, as I felt my balled fists loosen their grip, a low breath escaping my lips with a shudder. I twisted my head and caught a brief glimpse of our savior. Below, in a Sea Treader, was a familiar aged Wind Walker, hands raised, creating the constant gusts of wind that continued to cushion us from beneath as we descended, just enough so our bodies didn't end up crumpled and cratering on the hard deck of the Sea Treader when we landed—though not enough for there not to be unnerving pain from the impact, the air knocked from within us with a hiss and groan as the two of us tumbled into the Treader.

"Good timing, huh?" Elder Yinxing quipped, though there was a hard edge to her gaze, sharpening her usual sleepy expression.

"I had a feeling something like this might happen," Exile Song murmured, sheepish. He'd likely sent a message to call for help even before we stepped off the bridge with our sliders. He was always meticulous, level-headed—something I lacked.

"I've missed you," I said to Elder Yinxing as I stripped the tattered Feng cloak from my back. She pulled from a hidden storage compartment a white cloak embroidered with metallic copper accents, one that Zinc's most trusted followers wore, and handed it to me. She then grabbed another cloak for Exile Song. Now with the hoods of our cloaks up and drawn close, the three of us would look identical.

Sea Treaders were not too dissimilar to Travelers, except rather than legs, there were three bladed propellers at the back that resembled the fins of fish, and their bodies were longer, wider, in the shape of an elongated egg. There was no fur lining—at least not in this Treader, because Elder Yinxing had removed it the moment we'd gotten ahold of it after several guards had abandoned it, decommissioned, in the sea. The floor of the Treader was hard, cold, under my feet, and the seat, too, when I collapsed into it, was uncomfortable in its rigidity. I shifted, again and again, then gave up, because it only made me notice the texture of the Treader more.

I stared down at the cloak now wrapped around me, and even though it was only meant to be a disguise, my pores tightened uncomfortably at the texture of the fabric brushing against my shell. I should be used to it by now. This was not the first time I'd worn it.

"Thank you for coming," I said, and I meant it.

"Of course," Elder Yinxing said, restarting the Treader on standby, the bladed fins behind the vehicle propelling forth in the water. She could have brought a Shifter along, but that would warrant more notice than a Treader manually crossing the sea, as though it were simply a guard on watch, making their rounds.

I pulled the hood over my head as we moved towards Engine. The individual chambers, with both flat and turret roofs, protruded from the sides of the iron giant like multi-metallic colored bulbs, dull and blunted rather than shiny and polished, with scales that took form of the tiles on top of each—blue, red, purple, green. Just like the thick-trunked trees that flowered during the fall back in Feng. The iron giant was like a constructed version of the home I'd left—tame rather than unruly, yet still so deeply rooted in the mountain it had settled upon, carved out of the peak to fill with its own manufactured organs in the form of the experimental chambers alongside the ones within which the Sun Cores were trapped.

Engine's uneven symmetry, to me, was entrancing, beautiful even, in the way the Cogs had built something so unnatural yet made it appear as though it belonged, as though it always had. The way Zinc's library balanced near the top. Right next to it, the slow turn of the Time Teller, with its waterfall cascading down the side, functioned to cool Engine's persistent heat, and to remind all those looking that time would always be moving forward—and yet, to me, it always seemed as though the water would one day halt in its seemingly eternal fall.

Steam and smog pumped from smaller individual and larger shared chimneys, making it seem as though Engine would erupt and implode at any given moment. The iron giant was a waiting geyser of smoke and melting iron, a destruction barely contained. Seeing it all only added to my persistent unease, threatening to spill the inferno tears I'd been desperately withholding.

My comscreen vibrated, and I pulled it from my robes. Projecting from its glass surface was an image of the library, the glass of its long, narrow doors seeming as though it was wavering from the reflection of shifting clouds within. There was a flicker of a shadow before the glass doors swung backwards and out strolled the Iron Alchemist. He was adorned in a white cloak with copper and gold embroidered designs stitched with metallic silk, and a violet flourish at each sleeve and lining the collar. Zinc was ready for the Cogs, and one by one they clambered out of their creaking homes and onto their rooftops, though some remained hidden within their chambers or hung out of windows. A part of me shuddered at the sight of unquestioned obedience, but it was an echo of myself, of my sisters, who all followed Grandmother's will without truly understanding why.

On my screen I could see the Cogs staring towards Zinc in an unsteady, entranced way, waiting for his much-anticipated announcement. I wanted to look away, but pity swelled within me, forcing my gaze to linger. It brought to my mind the last speech he'd given, always words with fabricated evidence, fitting only the story he himself wished to tell.

The gods are misguided, but we will be here to direct them on the right path once more, and if they refuse, then we will be here to smother their challenge.

10

SANGSHU
THE ETERNAL BRIDGES

Engine's waterfall poured like straight-edged lighting strikes as we neared, the Treader drifting just close enough so we could use the rising mist for cover, but not so close we'd be sunken by the immensity and pressure of the tumbling water from above. I couldn't remember the last time it had rained—at least not on this side of the wall, though it was uncommon in Feng as well.

Feng only got drifting showers carried from afar from Glace—a hidden place that seemed to live within a perpetual gentle storm. Here, on this side of the wall, the closest thing to rain was the controlled flow of steam and smog from the chimneys and the salty mist of the water wheel mixed together—thick and uncomfortable. Yet both Feng and Engine were like an infinite puzzling of roots and hollows with its own river falling from the sky.

I stared first at the speck that was Zinc, waiting in front of the library doors.

Below the Time Teller, the library, the homes of all the Cogs, rested chambers for the production of luxuras, the same ones I'd seen hovering, staggered, on my way down to where Blinking Star and the other Sun Cores were held, overheating the exterior iron of Engine's body from downwards up so it required a constant stream to cool. It was a heat, a constant threat, that Zinc never had to worry about because its destruction would reach him last; by then, he would've already fled, leaving the rest of the iron giant he'd built to suffer the flames. Perhaps this was what he had wanted all along, an excuse to abandon another failed creation, to forget it had ever existed. But he didn't know that if Engine fell, it would not fall alone—that it would take Feng, Glace, with it, too: the very places he sought for future refuge and to conquer.

Elder Yinxing was first to step from the Treader when we docked below the squat mountain, the bottom of which flattened out into a short stretch of plains with water gently pushing against where it disappeared into the sea. The elder waited for Exile Song and me to disembark and directed us towards a shadowed area, behind the water cascading down from the Time Teller above. A few brown-cloaked figures awaited our arrival. We clustered near a wall, and Engine's searing heat radiated from its surface. We were careful not to touch the corroveins that extended outwards from the iron giant, spidering across the hard, unpaved ground.

The brown-cloaked Walkers tensed as we neared.

"Where—?"

"Did Zinc—?"

"—the rebels—"

In hushed whispers, Elder Yinxing explained the situation in Breath.

Behind me, Exile Song shadowed at a proximity I wouldn't have allowed anyone else. His cloak brushed mine, the gentle collision caressing my shell beneath.

As a uniformed collective, the Walkers watched as Elder Yinxing borrowed winds that grew in a dense swirl, preparing to lift us up the side of Engine towards Bronze's chamber, where we would be able to take refuge for now.

Copper had prepared us to be leaders, when we'd always been better followers—I'd hoped it would remain that way, but that, much like unwithheld trust, became an impossibility.

A light touch from Exile Song landed on my cloaked shoulder. "I will bring Lufeng back," he said.

"Be careful," I said, with my back turned, resisting the urge to stop him.

Exile Song brushed my back with his sleeve. I turned without looking, fixing my eyes on the ground instead.

Then, with a slight breeze, his touch left me. "I will." His words were in Song—a quiet, lulling trickle. For a moment, I closed my eyes and allowed the sound to linger. Outside of his gentle nature, what I loved most about Exile Song was his voice, and the steadfast quality of it that I desperately lacked. I used to have it back in Feng, when silence, stillness, came easy and natural.

It might be difficult to believe, and it certainly was for me, but Exile Song had also once been one of Zinc's closest guards.

"Why did you leave him?" I asked Exile Song when we'd first met at the Palace.

His voice had been a low hum, an answer in Song that might have sounded like a simple one-toned tremor to those unfamiliar with the language, but to me, it was a layered, rich-held timbre note of resonance. "He stopped trusting me."

As soon as Zinc ceased to offer it—trust, that is—others around him no longer felt the need to return it. I didn't ask what had made Zinc lose trust in Exile Song, and I was certain the answer didn't matter, because I understood paranoia would be Zinc's greatest downfall should he allow it to consume him—and it had. Though he held onto it as though it were his greatest strength.

It became clear to me why Zinc had such difficulties now with trust—because of all those who'd left him behind. It must have been such a lonely feeling. Sometimes, I wondered if Grandmother felt the same.

Before Exile Song reboarded the now empty Treader, his back turned, came the words in Song—a low resounding hum, pulsing, slow, like a whale call in the kind of depth where the water was so still that the sound of movements were muffled, as though time there had turned viscous.

"I missed you... too."

11

SANGSHU

BRASS'S HOME

Elder Yinxing helped propel me upwards, along the body of Engine, using gusts of borrowed wind. She followed close below. Beneath, the brown-cloaked figures watched our ascent with hoods up, heads tilted backwards. It felt both familiar and foreign every time I travelled this way, because the sensation was intimate, yet because I wasn't the one in control, it also felt distant. It made me miss the way I used to be able to call upon wind, feel its caress both beneath my feet and running through my fingers, waiting for a gentle, whispered request. We passed several chambers protruding outwards from the iron giant, careful to avoid the ones with open windows or with Cogs settled upon the rooftops until we slowed, before halting altogether at the home of the

Cog, Bronze: the one who convinced me to leave the rebels, and the place where I'd also first met Copper's daughter, Brass.

Elder Yinxing slowed our ascent, landing first herself, hidden beneath the shadows of the falls, near the rooftop of that familiar chamber, before depositing me next to her. Though my limbs had felt weightless only moments before, as soon as Elder Yinxing's borrowed wind left me, my body was suddenly heavy: each movement, at least at first, felt like moving through sand. Elder Yinxing's eyes, wise, weary, but with a comforting calmness, shifted around the shadowed area of the narrow tiling.

I was first to step from the shadows towards the edge of the rooftop. With light steps, I trod across the tiles with my cloak over my head. Below, inside the chamber, was where I'd hidden when I first fled from Zinc, the lingering effects of my self-alchemy burning up a fever—not unlike the one Brass herself was suffering when I tumbled into her home.

She, too, had been collapsed on the ground.

Core fever—from the rising heat in Engine, sped up by the impact of the corroveins.

That was also when I'd discovered how most Cog bodies were not strong enough to live outside of regulated environments.

"Are you with my mother?" Brass had asked me with fire in her eyes, even though her gaze was bleary from the fever. I didn't have the heart to tell her no, and when I finally had a chance to give her the answer she sought, she was no longer there to hear it. In her stead was a corpse, glassy eyes unblinking, staring at me with a withered gaze, as if asking what took me so long.

At that moment, I, too, wondered, why it had taken me so long. I knew this was a question Copper had also asked herself, as had Zinc, yet this same question spurred them on entirely different paths. And I suppose that was one of the reasons why I worked for Copper now. Out of regret. Out of guilt. Out of gratitude. Because of the mercy I'd been shown, the selflessness of a single Cog who made me believe there may be others, and there were, so many, who followed—Nickel and others who had placed themself in danger for Blinking Star and the Sun Cores countless times. And my hidden motive of saving Engine so Feng and Glace, everywhere Grandmother's roots reached, would also survive.

Yet there was an ache within me at the thought of the briefness of Cog lives, their fragility, their vulnerability. Perhaps one day I would come to regret the mercy I'd allowed myself to harbor, hoping that it would spur even the smallest of changes.

Just like Cog minds, I found Natural Engine and Titan minds difficult to decipher.

Mine was no exception.

Exile Song once asked me if Copper and I were not just obligatory allies, but also friends. Then he laughed in that deep, slow, pulsing way of his and added, "And us?" That, too, was a question I didn't answer, because the inferno tears within me caused the constant awareness that I was now a being too fleeting to hope for forever.

I ran a hand along each tile marked in Script—the names of those who once lived within the home, much like the way the trees in Feng were scarred when a Wind Walker passed. I wondered if that custom was derived from Engine, or if it was the other way around. Intangible culture like this wasn't recorded in the library—or perhaps it was lost—or perhaps it was a story Zinc and his ancestors had destroyed.

I spotted Brass's engraving, passed at twenty-five annuals. Brass was so similar to her mother, to her uncle, Zinc, but she also reminded me, now, of Lufeng. Though it might be more accurate to say that Blinking Star reminded me of Brass, in her headstrong nature and defiance. There were many Cogs like her.

I reached the roof's edge, kneeled, hands gripping the tiles to keep myself from tipping over, and looked under. The window was open, only a sliver. I reached a hand down, knocked, a specific pattern that Exile Song had taught me, like the periodic fall of a single drop of rain from the tip of a leaf the dawn after a storm.

Bronze looked up, startled, mouth held agape like a fish on land. Their cheeks had that same hint of the telltale crimson of core fever causing the blood vessels beneath their skin to swell.

Then familiarity creased Bronze's expression, melting the fear into relief. I lifted a finger to my cracked lips while holding Bronze's gaze before beckoning Elder Yinxing forward. I swung from the rooftop through the window of the chamber. In the corner of the rather barren room was a bundled quilt, worn but colorful.

"Thank you for your service," I whispered.

In a small voice, Bronze responded, "Of course."

My core stuttered at their voice, the sight, the memory, the melancholy I thought I'd left behind.

Bronze was quick to close the window behind us when I waved for them to do so as soon as Elder Yinxing made her way inside after me. From the slight slanted openings of the window, I surveyed the layered homes of Engine around this one. There were more windows and doors that remained shut compared to before, Cogs on rooftops with expressions more defiant than docile. Within, I allowed the swell of hope to simmer, then I smothered it, because this was just the beginning.

12

LUFENG

CRAWLING VEINS

I ran a hand along the strange veins lining the tracks and crates—something that seemed to plague both the bridges and Engine itself, as though the iron giant were struggling against the festering of disease. A dying storm tree that eventually felled. I had asked Grandmother if we could save it, asked the healers to revive the tree. She had told me that nothing that was already rotten at its roots could be recovered. And yet, I had sat with the fallen tree, its dark bark eventually became ashen, before disappearing altogether.

"How do you plan to destroy Engine?" I asked.

"Corroveins. We've been infecting Engine and the bridges with it for a while now. Just one last large-scale push and the iron giant will fall," said Fog.

Fog explained the rebels' discovery of rust—the way

Wind Walkers and Water Shifters working together could create seemingly harmless moisture from the combination of breath and water that would oxidize the iron giant's skin, eating until it fell into nothing but scattered terracotta ashes. I thought again of the storm tree that had passed, and even given my scorn for Zinc and Engine, a part of me found its impending destruction pitiful. I could not help but imagine the Cogs sitting next to their fallen home, as though waiting for it to piece itself back together, re-erect itself from its own rusted ashes.

"There is one issue. Copper is trying to stop us, and your sister is helping her."

"Sangshu?" I asked, confused.

"If you mean Waiting Sun, then yes," Fog said, a frown pulling down his lips. "She's trying to help Copper save Engine, undo our damage, but its structure has already been weakened. Even without us, it will collapse on its own eventually. But we don't have time to wait for them to become the cause of their own destruction when so many of us have died for it already."

Fog paced, and the rest of the rebels' attentions were fixated on his even movement. I grimaced at the sight because it reminded me of Zinc and his guards.

But I could not help but be persuaded by Fog's words. The Land Wanderers, the Cogs: they may live a hundred years, but we could live for thousands. And yet, they had sliced our lifespans shorter than their own; uprooted saplings before they even had a chance to tower.

"Your sister. Waiting Sun. She's selfish. She wants us to sacrifice ourselves to *help* the Cogs. To cleanse Engine of the corroveins so that it remains standing. So we all remain under their control."

But that did not make sense. Sangshu would not do such a thing, would not save Engine, after all Zinc had done to Feng and our family—would she?

I rationalized aloud. "The photograph on the comscreen I saw back in the Palace, her escape. She—"

"—betrayed us," the rebel Current interrupted. "We fear she might be aligned with Zinc as well."

Fog's actions became more frantic, laced with urgency, as he pulled out a comscreen. Hovering from it was a photograph.

It was Sangshu, standing next to Zinc, both adorned in the glorious white robes of the Palace. It could not be her, yet it was. Both of them wore smiles that seemed eerily similar. My mind both urged me to reach forth and grab the comscreen from Fog, to stare at Sangshu's image and find evidence that it was not her, just someone who looked like her, and at the same time, I could not bring myself to look closer, just in case what Fog said was true.

The unspoken word 'death' lingered heavy and dense in the air between us, seeming to draw the breath from my body, leaving me with quiet, shallow gasps.

I swallowed the thought that compared Fog now to Zinc, how his actions felt like a different kind of manipulation, only for a cause that I, too, believed in.

The rebels wanted me to be merciless, to see the Land Wanderers and Cogs as the enemy, just as they saw us as the same. And perhaps that was the only option left. Perhaps it was too late to see them as anything else.

That was when I noticed a familiar face, Exile Song's, hidden in the crowd. A hope swelled within me—that perhaps he could tell me that everything Fog had said about Sangshu was false, that he could take me away so I would not have to bear the realities of our clashing words and the deaths it had wrought upon us all and would continue to in an endless cycle. Exile Song caught my eye and offered the slight shake of his head. But regardless of whether joining the rebels was the right choice, if they could even be trusted, they had Chuiliu and Changqing.

I looked down, refusing to look at Exile Song again as I offered my answer to the Current. Maybe there was only a single answer that could end this all.

"Very well," I said. "What do you need me to do?"

13

SANGSHU
THE IRON ALCHEMIST

As I paced the Cog's chamber, awaiting news from Exile Song, I listened to the loud rush of the Time Teller's waterfall right outside. The constant motion of the giant device contrasted with how seemingly slow time passed in Feng—the way time didn't seem to matter on the other side of the wall.

Here, every second that passed was laced with a fear that it was being wasted. Every breath inhaled and exhaled harbored the fear of an uncertain end. How finite time was and how easy it would be to lose track of it if the water ever halted, if the wheel ceased to spin, if the sea became a drained land of drought instead of its constant and almost soothing, even if at times terrifying, motion. There were so many things out of the Cogs' control.

Exile Song had asked why I chose to perform such an alchemy of flesh on myself, and at the time, I didn't know how to respond.

Perhaps it was because I'd lost my wind affinity, knew I couldn't ever get it back, not unless I returned to Feng. For some reason, I believed I never could, or perhaps I feared returning. Or maybe I knew I was needed more on the other side of the wall than in Feng, given the information Grandmother had trusted me with.

Regardless, I thought in changing my flesh, I would be able to feel again, maybe something like the way the Cogs feel. Perhaps I could experience a different kind of fear or fill the emptiness within: I wasn't sure. I wondered if that was how Cogs felt all the time—uncertain. It was terrifying, but also exhilarating, to experience what it was like to fear time running out, to be propelled forth, driven to action, by that same fear—even if aimless, even if sometimes mistakenly and impulsively.

It was a dangerous way to live, but it also offered a peculiar experience of life—one present and immediate rather than dulled and lingering.

From my comscreen, I watched as Zinc directed his words to the mass of collected Cogs staring at him with glazed eyes, mesmerized as though they were hearing messages from divinity itself. "The gods always take back what they have given."

For a moment, I wondered if Zinc knew the truth about Grandmother, about her connection to Engine, to Feng, to Glace. Or was he simply spouting lies once more.

In the end, my mind settled on the latter. It stirred within me the rise of anger in the form of bubbling inferno tears collecting, coming to the beginnings of a boil, even though I should be used to Zinc and his edged speeches.

The way Zinc spoke to others outside the quiet confines of the library, when we shared whispered conversations over texts and alchemy, was jarringly different. In the alchemy chamber, his speech was at times solemn, reminding me of Grandmother, and at times eager like a curious child. In front of the Cogs—outsiders—he carefully constructed a figure to hide his true nature, as though the sides of him he'd revealed to me never existed. And it made me wonder which was his reality—the one speaking to Lufeng now or the mentor who had guided me in the past.

"Now I know the gods are not such immortal beings, such untouchable things," Zinc continued. "We can reach the gods, and we could take them down. We can *control* and *conquer* them. We can live… among them, with them, *as* them, but now, *without* them and without having to *become like them*. For years we've suppressed the lesser and minor beings of the Natural Engines, but today… *today*, I hold news much better than anything you've ever anticipated."

A sharp intake of breath and murmurs spread in waves across the listening Cogs, an insistent humming that made it seem as though the iron giant itself was speaking in an ancient language no one could decipher.

Most couldn't come to terms with reality until they saw the shadows that had been spreading beneath the light. But what if we were only shown a false light with hands clutching at our shoulders, making sure we could never turn to look even at our own shadows—much less the ones cast by others, by Engine, by Zinc?

I asked Copper once why she didn't simply reveal the truth to the Cogs. *I've thought about it, but words, images, could only go so far if the Cogs have not witnessed themselves nor experienced the truth behind their fidelity to Zinc.* This was something I, too, thought about, when considering revealing my grandmother's rooted connections to Copper, and again when I decided against it. Sometimes truth was better withheld; sometimes if revealed, there was an opportunity for it to be weaponized. Yet, it could be the case that Copper already knew and was using the knowledge as leverage to save her own home. It could be the very reason she approached me. I couldn't blame her even if it were the case.

Though Copper was attempting to undo the harm Zinc had caused by working with Aunt Xiangmu, Grandmother, and the beings of Glace, neither Zinc nor Copper were willing to meet one another in the middle. The pair always spoke at and over one another, never truly having a conversation, a two-way discussion. And they left the rest of us to deal with the fallout of their individual war. I'd joined the rebels originally, believing that ending it all would be better than searching for a solution, that attempting a war to end all wars was the answer to it all.

Everyone was speaking, but no one was listening.

Except, perhaps, the Cogs. All they'd ever done was listen. At least, a good many of them.

I watched the Cogs, adept at giving Zinc the attention he craved. Zinc had a certain charisma that elicited the trust of others, making them feel special, putting on an act of being likeable, capable but not threatening, even slightly dim in his projected idealistic ambitions, so others might be less wary, overlook or ignore what the Iron Alchemist tried to hide—only to make betrayal that much easier.

Behind Zinc was a follower with their cloak-drawn head dipped. Zinc turned to address the mystery follower.

I read each word his lips formed, only a mumble for Cogs who weren't looking too closely, something meant only for those watching for something specific—for *me* to notice. *"Is she here?"*

I caught a glimpse of the follower beneath the cloak—Tin, the Tasker I'd met back at the Palace—who whispered back with a hand held to her mouth, concealing her answer. Back at the Palace, Tin was a figure lingering in Zinc's shadow, always attempting to garner the master alchemist's attention and approval to no avail. For that, she always bore a grudge against me. I'd heard she'd succeeded, after I'd left. Only to be cast away whenever Zinc saw fit. It seemed, at this moment, Tin had his favor. Perhaps even begged her way into it.

My eyes narrowed, as though the act could help me see through Tin's upheld sleeve, through her flesh, decipher what it was she didn't want others to know. Zinc smiled in response, amused, his face taking on a fervent glow, making him almost ethereal.

The Iron Alchemist refocused his attention on the audience, staring directly into an onyx watcher—the dark orbs like the pupils of eyes, surveillance devices to overwatch where Zinc couldn't be physically present—as though it were his long-lost lover before continuing his speech. "The natural gods have turned their backs on us."

It was untrue, but it didn't matter what was being said, only who was saying it. As Zinc took a step backwards, for a moment I anticipated Lufeng being brought forth by the guards. That Zinc had somehow stolen her back from the rebels. That he was sure to make of her an example of how the gods, the Natural Engines, could be controlled.

It was sickening the way he glorified us and yet in

the same breath cast us as antagonists, the way the Iron Alchemist had always preyed on our naivety, continued to prey. I couldn't believe that at one point, I, too, desired Zinc's favor, and perhaps it was because I had been so angry at Grandmother for sacrificing me and the rest of our family. I was too young to understand back then, and even now, I felt too young to understand anything fully, or truly at all.

I waited and waited, but Lufeng never stepped into the onyx watchers' eyes. I checked my messages again, to quell the uneasy stirring of the inferno tears within, but there was still no communication from Exile Song, even with the flood of messages from the others, asking if it was yet time to gather.

Not yet.

There was a long pause as more onyx watchers collected in front of the Iron Alchemist, but I should've already understood that silence was far more dangerous than storm. Heat prickled beneath my hardened surface, and I willed the rising anxiety to rest, calm.

The onyx watchers drifted through the sky like eclipsed moons, so small they could easily fit into a Land Wanderer's or Cog's palm, yet the longer I stared, the more the orbs started to resemble the Cogs' pupils, without the whites nor irises. Instead of a chill, water vapors from the surrounding air sizzled against my shell. I winced, not from the slight discomfort of the pain, but from the coldness of where the vapor met my skin.

Then, I felt every fissure across my body tighten as Zinc stared into the onyx watcher and smiled directly at me. Or at least, that was how it felt.

There was no time to dwell on that thought because only a moment later the collected onyx watchers in front of Zinc scattered across Engine, projecting a series of moving images: Lufeng's attempt at taking Father's life at the 'ceremony,' her escape from the Palace, her breaking of the contract, her 'stealing' her sibling and fleeing to Feng. Then, it flickered to Exile Song charging through the Palace with the Traveler, Lufeng being whisked upon it, their stampede towards the window, focusing in on *her* destruction, the ferocity of her rage warped from something courageous to an expression that took on a terrifying tone—glare wild, mouth snarling, hair a tangled disarray like a nest of snakes.

The plunge of the Traveler towards the sea with Lufeng and Exile Song, along with the two saplings, stuttered and disappeared, and in its place was Lufeng next to a handful of rebels adorned in their grey cloaks billowing in the smoke at the base of Engine.

Whether the rebels themselves predicted this outcome or not, this was the exact progression of events Zinc sought, and I wouldn't be surprised if he had shaped it all, moving the pieces, underhandedly spurring the rebels on, so they collided according to his will.

"You see now, the Natural Engines are bent on

destroying our homes, destroying *us*, so naturally we must take theirs." Every word that left Zinc's lips was followed by projected images of Feng and Glace from the onyx watchers scattered across Engine, positioned in front of groups of Cogs watching from their rooftops and windows.

For Zinc, there had always been two options—the abandoned first: *become them, the gods, the Natural Engines*; the second: *take over their homes.* Now it was clear he only had one.

It seemed Zinc's plan had always been to show he had conquered the gods and had always been working towards moving to the other side of the wall—a slow trade of places so he could enjoy an untouched haven while we reckoned with impending disaster. But Zinc would only turn Feng and Glace into mirrors of Engine given enough time—industrialize the lands, make them into iron homes, even though the first attempt, Engine, inherited from his ancestors, was falling, dying.

"Grace your eyes upon our new homes."

I'd remained with Zinc for as long as I had because a part of me agreed, and still did, with Zinc's original intent: why it was necessary for him to attempt terraforming the world to suit the Cogs' needs, turning unpredictable landscapes into gears and engines.

Zinc had told me his first father passed at sea, swallowed by the waves; that his second father was lost in the terracotta dunes of Clay, his body droughted when he was finally found; that his first mother perished in the mountains on which Engine rested, hunted by wild predators who inhabited the caves and hid among the roots of trees; and his second mother suffered a different type of corroveins, ones that ate at her organs and flesh rather than at iron and other metals. He had told me he wished to protect those weakest in the face of nature, and yet it seemed as though it was something he'd abandoned altogether. Or perhaps he had only said all these things to sway my loyalties.

If I had been born a Cog, perhaps I would have gone down the same path as Zinc.

In the Iron Alchemist's eyes now shone the very words he told me were his ironclad worldviews: Everything is replaceable, disposable—like the Natural Engines, the Natural Titans, Glace, Feng, Clay, Gear, Engine. All of it.

The final words of his broadcast rang loud and clear:

"Our new world has arrived—and it is time for us to enter."

These final words held the weight of generations, standing for continuous cycles of rise and collapse, repeating until the day where nothing could be made again from the ashes. Only Zinc had not realized that the being enduring each cycle rise and collapse would fall with his master plan, taking with her everything he wished to keep, leaving behind nothing for him to stand upon in victory and rule.

14

SANGSHU

ENGINES AND TITANS

The fall of water from the Time Teller, mixed with the rumble of inferno tears flowing within me, became too loud to my ears. Bronze's chamber felt crowded even though the three of us—Bronze, Elder Yinxing, and me—stood a comfortable distance apart from each other. Steam clouded my mind, seething through my temples. My thoughts churned with a dizzying warmth, constant, a swirling gust of wind, an endless number of conclusions breathing in and out like the information that muddled the minds of each Cog within Engine, rendering them in a state of confusion of which they themselves were unaware.

The space around me felt suspended for a moment before I was plunged back into the present. Bronze shifted, unsettled from the corner of the metallic chamber.

Then, a message came from Exile Song—*The rebels are coming. Terracotta Dune has evacuated the Palace and will be joining those on Gear to slow down the rebels.*

My hands shook as I sent a mass message to all of Terracotta Dune—Copper's—supporters: *Prepare for corrovein eradication and rebel counter.*

Copper's words pounded to the hissing of steam billowing the sleeves and body of my cloak—*You want to save your home? Then do not give Zinc a reason to invade it.* I felt the festering eruption within me prodding beneath the surface, attempting to escape through the fissures, prying tendrils of smoke and steam in hopes of widening the minuscule pathways.

Not yet—

—not yet.

I pulled down my hood, allowing free the tendrils of my hair the texture and state of smoke, the color of loose snow gathered and tainted by ashes. Elder Yinxing and I prepared to head for where the Eternal Bridges met the center of Engine, entrances Cogs used to be able to access, now blocked off and used only for the import and export of goods between Gear and Engine. We told Bronze to evacuate everyone, both allies and those against us, from Engine to the underground refuge beneath the iron giant that the alchemists before Zinc had built in case of disaster, but left unused for many, many annuals.

I sent a message to Blinking Star, hoping she'd

managed to free all the Sun Cores by now, just in case Engine did fall.

Soon, Exile Song, Elder Yinxing, and I would be stationed at the mouth of each bridge, positioning groups composed of Natural Engines and a Natural Titan—a Water Shifter, an Oric, and a Wind Walker—or Titan pairings of an Oric and a Current—where sections of corroveins ran most rampant along the foundation of the iron giant and its tongues, the bridges. Some groups and pairings would remain at the Wheels and Churners of Gear or along the bottoms of the belts, regrouping with Copper to halt the rebels in their path to bombard the iron giant.

That should have been how the mobilization proceeded, but nothing had ever gone according to our initial, or even backup, plans. We were always one step behind, simply reacting to the situations we were presented with, unable to predict Zinc's volatility and inconsistency. Now even the rebels were acting much like Land Wanderers and Cogs in their emotionally spurred acts.

Not long after the message was sent out to everyone under our command, Water Shifters, Wind Walkers, and Currents broke from their stations in Gear—a great risk they were taking, for it was obvious they were all contracted by Zinc, families held as hostages by ink and Script, though it didn't matter to them now, because they were willing to sacrifice it all to save

Engine, knowing already what it would mean should it fall—coming in swarms across all three of the Eternal Bridges, under or as part of the waves, carried by the wind, or a merger of the two as those who lost their affinities relied on those who hadn't. From different hiding places—some among the cliffs below the Palace, some in the mountains beneath Engine, some out of the forests on Gear, and from the confines of Copper's sectors between the Time Teller and nested beneath the cover of the falls—came the Natural Titans.

Copper always said the best place to hide was where the opposing end would never expect, and where we could closely monitor the enemy; where we were able to, quite literally, reach them at less than a single shell crater's length.

Yet, too many flooded from Gear and from hiding. The rebels were on the move. We only had to move faster.

With the help of Elder Yinxing, I made my way out of Bronze's chamber and down to the base of Engine. We positioned ourselves at the mouth of each Eternal Bridge, staring down the long stretches connected to Gear, ready to welcome and oversee the Natural Engines and Titans who passed us like a gathered colony of bees, a blend of water and currents, bark and needle threads, what I imagined our world would look like from above if the wind carried us high enough to look down below, with a singular goal in mind.

As those commanded by me and Elder Yinxing took their stations, those under Exile Song perfectly positioned themselves even without their leader, who I hoped would soon join them. A low burning grew uncomfortably within me at the thought of Exile Song's prolonged absence. He should have been back by now. With Lufeng. With Chuiliu and Changqing.

Behind, the corroveins along Engine's body slowly dissolved, receding as the Orics retched from their bodies the acid they had been infused with and contained within them, seeming as though large slivers of their flesh had been sliced and removed as offerings. The thicker liquid wove with the Water Shifters and Currents carried upwards from the surrounding sea in tumbling waves, flung towards Engine's walls by gusts of wind borrowed by the Walkers and Currents. Each time the mixture of water and oric crashed against the iron giant, a low groaning echoed outward, trembling up and down the metal, painful moans of Engine struggling to barely hold on against the opposing assault of both the rebels and allies of Copper.

However, not all the Orics were able to separate the acid from their bodies. Some tore themselves apart—rather than slivers, they sliced open their flesh, allowing the outpour of the currents held within their bodies, the way sap leaked from Wind Walkers, blood from Land Wanderers and Cogs. Their eyes were the last things to be seen, blinking rapidly until they closed forever. As each of these Orics dissolved, the acidity of their bodies became laced with the waters carried and spread further by the Wind Walker and Currents, washing over the body of the iron behemoth. It was as though I were watching a cycle of death and rebirth happening right before me—copper ashes, rust decay, flaking like sands of terracotta dunes disintegrating from the grey metal body of Engine.

It was both beautiful and tragic.

Footage from Gear, the bridges, and around Engine flooded onto my comscreen. Some groups disappeared along with the corroveins, and I forced my eyes to remain open to watch their sacrifice, their willing deaths—all knowing exactly what would happen if Engine were to fall, if Grandmother's roots within the mountains collapsed with it.

Yet, even as we dissolved the corroveins, stripping them from the body of Engine, a sense of dread chilled me. It was the first time since becoming a Sun Core that I had felt true cold.

A familiar mist, quickly thickening and becoming fog rising from the sea, slid along the bridge that should have been commanded by Exile Song. It was the same fog that had appeared when Lufeng was intercepted, the same fog that the rebels used to mask their corrovein infiltrations.

The fog darted forth at an unnatural speed, one clearly controlled, and I realized it was in fact warm steam. Its heat overwhelmed me in its path to swallow the iron giant. I didn't need to turn to know that the rust we'd sacrificed so many to cleanse would outpace our efforts. Before she even appeared from the steam, I already prepared myself for the collision.

15

LUFENG

A CHAMBER ON ENGINE

As I travelled towards Engine with the rebels, led by Fog, most propelled forward by Walkers borrowing wind, Fog tasked me with bringing down my own sister.

I swallowed the bitter thought of confrontation as we drew farther from Gear, surrounded by rebels who had left their stations at the Wheels and Churners—many of whom were halted by others like themselves, who appeared to be on Sangshu and Copper's side.

"How will I find her?" I asked.

"You will," Fog said.

"How—?"

Fog was already off before I could enquire further, speeding towards Engine with a swarm of rebels behind him, while I was falling behind.

Before I made it to the bridge, floods of Wind Walkers, Water Shifters, and Currents entered into struggles with the opposition, blown off course by fervent winds or pressed into the sea by swallowing waves. I whipped around, attempting to catch hold of a being, any being, as one by one those around us were intercepted, pulled from the sky. I watched with horror, withdrawing into myself as they tumbled towards the waters.

In the distance, beings like Exile Song, Orics, were trying to reduce the impact of Fog's allies, attempting to rid the iron giant of rust before it could grow further. Rage flared within me, then confusion, at why the Natural Engines and Titans were working against one another. The Orics extracted the acid from the controlled rivulets within their bodies, wove it with the water that the Shifters and Currents were guiding towards Engine, or merged themselves in their entirety with the rising sea as sacrifices. It pained me to see so many perish for the sake of the iron giant, for the Cogs, and Fog's quiet and solemn expression told me that this was no surprise.

The rebel watched, expression grim and anticipatory, as if waiting for something specific. Again, a weary prickle scattered at the back of my neck at the potential that Fog was withholding something important from me. But all of this became secondary: I had to find Sangshu before Fog would tell me where Chuiliu and Changqing were.

I was not sure how I would be able to locate Sangshu, but there was no time to shape a coherent plan as the flurry of rebel Natural Engines and Titans pushed me forth towards Engine. Pressure surged against me from all sides, sometimes disappearing for seconds as an Engine or Titan was intercepted, before their presence was quickly replaced by another rejoining or forging ahead in the crowd. It was impossible to do anything except move forward, because each motion felt like an attempt to find an impossible break in the rapid rise and recession of waves breaking against a shore.

A hand darted out and grabbed hold of my arm, withdrawing me from the crowd as my limbs flailed and collided with several beings in the process, leaving parts of my bark nicked, the small, sliced wounds stinging. Just as I was about to voice my complaint, a hiss left my lips, and I noticed the person holding my arm was Exile Song.

The question that had been hovering persistently at the back of my mind flew from my mouth. “Do you know where Chuiliu and Changqing are?” I demanded, my voice a choked sob.

His troubled expression turned into a grimace; his lips pressed into a solemn line. “No… I am sorry,” he said.

I shook his hand from my arm. If he could not help me, then my only choice was to fulfill my bargain with Fog, turn his rage into my own, and hopefully at the end of all the carnage, my siblings would be returned to me.

I darted forward away from Exile Song. He followed as close as he could, carried forth by waves that he did not allow to touch his body, only the surface of his robes. My mind swirled with Zinc's words as they took root in every thought.

"Do not listen to them!" Exile Song shouted above the wind and the crash of waves around us. At first, I thought Exile Song meant Zinc before he continued, "The rebels."

"Then who should I fight for?" I shouted back, hands quivering as I willed the wind to drive me forth quicker and quicker towards Engine. "The Cogs fear us, envy us, and call us gods when all we ever were in their eyes is disaster—they see us as nature's retaliation. They're trying to smother us for the same reason," I seethed. "Isn't it only fitting that we destroy them with what they created with their own hands? We should remind them why they found us dangerous because it seems they have long forgotten."

"The rebels just want to use you to serve their own purposes." Exile Song was calm, but there was a firmness to his words.

"So you're on Copper and Sangshu's side." I laughed, the bitterness of the sound surprising me. "Then is that not what you are doing as well? In approaching me?"

"I—"

"What is the difference?" I whispered, tone cold, resolved.

"Zinc is allowing this because this is what he wants! How does this solve anything? Is this your definition of rebellion? Destruction? Is that what you think is the solution? To do exactly what *they're* doing?" Exile Song asked. There was now a simmering fury in his eyes—it was the most unsettled I had ever seen him.

"She's using you, too," I said, resisting the urge to withdraw in the intensity of Exile Song's stare.

He looked away, and I took a shuddering breath as he spoke. "No. I've decided this on my own."

"They would be gone—all of them. The Cogs," I whispered, and it sounded thunderous as we hovered in the wind, detached from the crowd moving forth only several gusts away with renewed fervor. Below, the Wind Walker who was keeping Exile Song afloat stared elsewhere, towards Engine.

I turned to see Exile Song shaking his head. "Is that what you really wish for?"

"Yes." I thought about the Wheels and Churners of Gear, of the uprooted grounds leading to the Palace, all the Wind Walkers who had disappeared through the gates, before settling on Chuiliu and Changqing, Mother and Father.

After a moment, Exile Song bowed his head with defeat. Or perhaps something else, because I could not see his expression.

"What do you wish for?" he whispered.

It was strange that he did not try to argue further, but at the same time, the Exile Song I knew was never one for conflict—more a silent, hidden defiance.

His eyes darted to the side, towards Engine, staring across the remaining stretch of the Eternal Bridges that had halted in their slow roll. Some of the crates were being knocked into the waters or set askew on the belt by the Engines and Titans travelling above and below. Amid the crowd, I had not noticed we were already halfway across the bridge. The distance we crossed, seemingly in seconds, seemed like an endless stretch. I followed Exile Song's stare.

A sharp breath left me as I saw a young Cog, and trailing behind them, all hand in hand along with the Cog, bundled in cloaks, were several young Wind Walkers and Water Shifters fleeing the groaning iron giant as it suffered the onslaught of rebel attack. My limbs quivered at the sight, because they all reminded me of my siblings. For a moment, I wished they were among them, just so it would calm my persistent worries concerning their whereabouts.

They headed towards a passage at the side of the mountain below Engine. A large metal door was already amid the process of sliding closed slowly to avoid the impending currents from flooding the interior while hopefully offering enough time for those still making their way to safety before the entrance was sealed. A wave crashed a little too close to the fleeing line: doubtless the next wave might knock them from their path. The iron giant rumbled, and though Exile Song and I remained steady, carried by the wind and water, the young Cog stumbled backwards. The Walker right behind them attempted to halt their fall and in the process tumbled onto the ground along with the young Cog, bringing down with them the trailing Walkers and Shifters. The next wave rose, looming over them on the ground.

Panicked, I attempted to dart towards them, but Exile Song held me back. Instead, he struggled to settle the water, still the waves, as the young Cog, Walkers, and Shifters scrambled up, scraping knees and hands in the process. The young Cog turned as they ran, saw us, and their expression smoothed to one of trust and relief, as though they were confident that we would save them. They were right.

"Go!" Exile Song and I shouted at the same time.

When the train disappeared behind the metal gateway almost closed, I went to follow, but again, Exile Song held me back and shook his head. "They will be alright."

"How could you trust them?" I asked as they disappeared behind the door. And yet, even as I asked this question, a part of me did exactly this—trust the young Cog, like I had with Brass, with Copper, with Nickel.

Is it not strange how a single being can chew through the seemingly impenetrable iron of our minds, through what we once held so tightly as the only truth within our lives? Does this make me fickle? Weak? Contradictory like the Cogs themselves? Is that such a terrible thing? I wanted to ask Exile Song. I wanted to know his answer.

"The same way you came to trust me," Exile Song said, quietly.

As I was about to respond, something from above caught my attention. Zinc. Drifting at the top of Engine. All thought flew from my head as I allowed my fury to fester. A thousand regrets engulfed me like a flame held to the branches of rooted trees who couldn't reach for escape. I had allowed myself to waver for a moment too long. Fog still had Chuiliu and Changqing, and I could not allow the virtue of one young Cog to sway me from my mission.

"Lufeng—"

With a gust of wind, I pushed Exile Song aside, almost knocking him down into the sea. I silently apologized before I propelled myself upwards, over the layered roofs of Engine, my feet barely brushing the surfaces. I now knew what the wind desired from us to wield it effortlessly. Trust. In the element. In ourselves.

When I reached Zinc, I rushed in front of him with an outstretched hand, grabbing his cloak, my fist at his neck.

"Coward," I whispered when I pulled Zinc's face close to mine. Yet instead of fear, there was a feverish excitement to his eyes drawn wide, as though he had been expecting me, as though I were just the guest he was seeking. Then, I shouted, louder, trying to withhold the tremor of my body from leaking into my voice.

"COWARD!"

16

SANGSHU

A COLLISON BELOW TIME

I heard a shout from above, a distant voice that somehow resonated from the top of Engine in an echoing thunder—Lufeng. She had borrowed the wind to carry her to the summit of Engine where Zinc still remained in front of the library.

My comscreen pinged—a message from Exile Song. I almost sighed in relief. But my attention was drawn back to Lufeng and Zinc, and I scrambled to locate Zinc's speech channel on my comscreen so I could catch their exchange. The onyx watchers continued to broadcast, following the pair closely as I watched the scene that unfolded above from below.

"COWARD!"

Lufeng seized Zinc by the robe, but he stepped

back from her grasp as easily as water slipping through collided boulders.

Zinc straightened his cloak and dusted it off as though it'd touched something filthy. "I think it's only fair for me to treat you with the same kindness you've shown us."

"You—"

Zinc held up a hand. "I'm sorry it has to be this way, truly. I am most apologetic."

Lufeng's voice echoed through the comscreen. "Apologies do not bring back the dead. Apologies are only the selfish acts of the living. You can utter them to your heart's content, but your words will only be carried by the wind and discarded, swept by rushing currents and carried downstream to a place no beings lay awaiting to listen."

The Iron Alchemist's expression was far too calm, even as Lufeng brought herself to a steady hover on borrowed wind, towering over Zinc.

At that moment, I was reminded of what Copper had once told me, *It is not those who voice their thoughts who are the most terrifying, it is those whose minds you cannot hope to read.*

The corroding foundation of Engine shrieked. The groan of the iron giant weakened with each passing second as its flesh was eaten by the rebels' Natural Engines and Titans. We were fighting a battle that would result in our sure loss with the rust growing and receding, growing and receding, but the gaps where the veins chewed off pieces of Engine were already beyond repair and were falling, tumbling into the waters below, swallowed completely by the sea.

"How does it feel? To have enclosing walls? To not be able to move past a boundary someone else has drawn?" Lufeng sneered, the wind gathered around her billowing her cloak behind.

It seemed everyone wanted to save their home, but everyone wanted to save their home their own way—even if it meant losing it altogether.

Even with all that was occurring, Zinc was smiling, as though this were all part of a hidden grand scheme.

Zinc retreated, whisking himself onto a Traveler, the guards that had caught up following behind, the iron talons of their machines plunging into the walls of Engine so they were almost horizontal, preparing for their descent. Then they disappeared on the comscreen. Moments later, I heard Zinc's voice again from above, directed not only at Lufeng but also at me.

"How does it feel? To have who you believed to be an ally turn on you?"

Then he was gone, and all that was left ringing in my ears was Lufeng's frustrated roar.

She had chosen her side, and I had chosen mine, and Zinc only had to wait and watch what was to come of the war fought between sisters who should have been working together, who shouldn't ever have had to fight to begin with.

He didn't care that the iron giant was crumbling, because he always had a backup plan in place. No. *This* was his plan all along. He *wanted* the rebels to destroy Engine because it would give him the very excuse to invade Feng and Glace. He'd already hidden everything he needed to rebuild a grander Engine, the ever-changing new world he'd always imagined, where the corroveins had no hopes of reaching—the Palaces, because rust couldn't penetrate bone.

Zinc and his ancestors had spent decades, centuries, digging into our very anatomy and psyches, while we never understood his mind, never truly, no matter how hard we tried to. The library held all written records of Natural Engines and now Titans, that I'd contributed to, foolishly, along with discoveries about our own natures that we ourselves were unaware of.

A voice hurtled from above me, echoing downwards: Lufeng's. "YOU!"

Seeing the vengeance in Lufeng's eyes made me understand how Zinc must have felt when he stepped into the library only to see an empty chamber and, in its wake, instead of his apprentice, a pile of ashes still blazing in an inferno.

I'd become a willing participant of this war the moment I welcomed the lure of alchemy, allowed it to cloud my judgment, to somehow make me forget I was experimenting with actual lives. Its addiction and the hunger for knowledge became an obsession. Until Zinc realized that perhaps it was better, after all, to keep all those around him ignorant if he wanted to control them.

So why, why was *I* chosen to receive the knowledge he held so tight?

Lufeng was the true answer as she knocked me against the side of Engine, driving me into the rusted iron walls with a loud *clang*—cracked ash solidified against flaking metal. My breath escaped me. The inferno tears within unsettled, quivering at my core from the impact. My head pounded, and heat continued to rise within my body, but Engine's own was already burning a higher fever. I turned my head to the side. The iron giant's slate-grey skin appeared to have taken on a crimson-tinged hue, like the scarlet-veined cheeks of Cogs suffering from core fever, like a bloody sun beneath a thick layer of mist and smoke—a red star that was waiting to set.

In a raging fury, Lufeng pinned me to the burning metal surface, the wind from her body and the smoke from mine intertwining—hers rippled dangerously while mine a low trail, hovering as if it too had breath that it held bated. Lufeng's forearm pinned my neck. In instinctive response, the fissures across my body tightened.

"Don't do this," I said. But Lufeng had always been

hard to bargain with, stubborn to a fault, not unlike my two other elder sisters. "The Cogs are only afraid because they don't understand. You know that."

"Do I? Have they ever tried to understand us?" Lufeng said, voice laced with scorn, pressing harder against my neck, choking the rising steam that struggled to escape at first but found release elsewhere throughout my body.

Darting through the air, I saw Fog spectating. The rebel leader had earned the trust of so many, yet no one knew his true name. Staring now at this victorious expression, I knew why Lufeng was behaving this way.

"We both know—there are those—who have and others—who never had—the chance to—most never had the—chance to," I said, sputtering, voice raised so Fog could hear. Then quieter, with minimal movement of my lips. "I know—where Chuiliu and Changqing are."

Engine groaned, creaked, and I could feel the walls shuddering against my back. I thought back to Zinc's smile. He would evacuate all the Cogs somehow, as difficult as it might seem given their home was on the verge of collapse. Or even if he didn't, he had followers elsewhere. Land Wanderers of Clay. He would never be left without a home nor without power.

Confusion clouded her face as she looked away, then her expression turned to one calculating, conflict brewing in the tense way she held her body, an internal war I'd never seen from my sister before. That was when she, too, spotted Fog before she turned back to me and mouthed, *Where are they?*

"Lufeng." Heat pulsed within me at the unfamiliar feeling of her name from my lips. One I had not uttered in a very long time.

She paused at her name, eyes widening, arm loosening her hold. "Who… are you?"

My throat dried, the inferno tears within me stilled, the sensation almost one of cooling ice, even though I knew it would be impossible with my body's current composition. It was the first time I had felt such a sensation, such coldness, since I'd been alchemized.

No, this wasn't a chill.

It was a searing heat at a temperature so high it could almost be mistaken as an arctic bite, the breath of death clutching at my core, at the collected inferno tears, deep within, until I realized that once I reached deep enough, it wasn't a dark coldness I'd touch but a smoldering fever that could be felt long before it could even be grazed—

—a different kind of Time Teller that served as a reminder that one day, long before any other being, I'd be burnt out and left scattered and alone.

17

LUFENG

A COLLISION ABOVE TIME

I dragged the Natural Titan, who seemed to be one of the leaders working for Copper, upwards, propelling us both to the top of Engine, away from the flurry of Walkers, Shifters, Currents and Orics, away from the eyes and ears of Fog. The Natural Titan was a being I had not seen before—with a cracked skin of white-grey like layered ashes, hair of smoke, swirling but never dissipating.

I clutched tight the cloak around their neck as I landed us on the open-space balcony, unrailed, of what I had been told by Fog was Zinc's library, right next to a large churning water wheel. When I let go of the Titan, I pushed them back with a gust of wind so strong they were almost knocked off the edge.

From their cloak fluttered a mask of dead driftwood

with familiar features—my fourth sister's. I tensed, eyes unshifting from the sight of Sangshu's discarded face, then I stared up at the Titan in front of me, eyes narrowing at her as I noticed each of her features with growing clarity—ashened skin with crawling fissures, crevices both dark and deep, with a few pulsing a dim amber from beneath. Her hair was no longer needle threads but tendrils of living smoke. Utterly unfamiliar.

"Sang… shu?" I dared to utter.

Surprise flashed across the Titan's face, then, a grimace, as skepticism and paranoia called question to my conclusion. Then, the guilt on her face was the confirmation I needed.

Sangshu. My sister, who now felt as though a stranger.

"Why?" I asked, voice low, almost drowned by the deep groaning cries of the Engine threatening to topple and the rampant waves below.

I wanted to ask her if she regretted her decision, and it seemed as though Sangshu read my mind as she looked away. There was no hesitation to her silent response. At this moment, she felt as though an unknowable, incomprehensible being.

My feet remained planted, unsure if I should remain here, or go after Zinc, or find Exile Song, when Sangshu shuffled forward from the edge where she stood with the stuttering flow of water behind her crashing down sporadically into the sea. She reached forth and tugged on the edge of my cloak the same way Chuiliu did, the same way Sangshu once had when we were both far younger. When we knew nothing outside of the storm trees that shielded us from the rest of the world.

I flinched the same moment she did, as if suddenly realizing her actions. Resounding within me was the type of betrayal that stunned most because it was from someone I wanted desperately to trust. Perhaps it was because we were family, perhaps it was because she reminded me, at this moment, of Chuiliu. But then I thought of Fog, of what he had said about Sangshu, her potential alliance with Zinc.

"Sister," Sangshu said, voice low. We were never close and yet, she stared at me wide-eyed as though she had mourned my missing presence for a long while.

I stared and stared because she was both someone I had been searching for a long while and someone I hoped I would never find.

Sangshu took a step back slowly, the action causing the edge of her cloak to catch on the creased sides and rough bark surface of the mask still on the ground by her feet. With the flick of her foot, she whisked it off the edge.

It fluttered, catching in the wind, before disappearing among the empty rooftops of Cog homes and the turret points of chambers. The Cogs, the thousands inhabiting Engine, must have completed their evacuation. Exile

Song had assured me that there were emergency shelters built within the mountains beneath Engine. If I could not trust him, I knew not who else I could trust.

Peering down the side of Engine, below, the corroveins spurred onwards by the rebels chewed even faster, darting up the iron giant that could do nothing but sit, awaiting its own death. The chambers of the Cog homes protruding from the side of Engine swayed precariously; some had already fallen, crashing down into the sea below, carried away by the waves, bobbing, buoyant like large, colored cradles.

This had been my dream since entering the Palace, since realizing the reality of Zinc and his plans and his creations—to witness his downfall, the crumble of his home; yet, this solution, a dangerous idealization that I had so naively held onto, echoed within me.

I never truly understood what this really meant, perhaps not even now, as I began to second-guess all it was that the rebels stood for, all that I thought I had unwavering faith in when I had spotted Zinc. The reality of Feng, of Glace, of the wall, of Gear and Engine resting beyond it, was something that continued to change, that was ever shifting within my mind, to a point I no longer knew what I knew and what I did not, what was truly right or wrong, because a part of me knew there was something that no one was telling me, or perhaps, there was something everyone thought I already knew.

I had to make a decision. I stared hard at my sister, begging her in silence to change my mind, to offer me another option, and to give me the courage to act upon it.

"Chuiliu and Changqing," I croaked. "Where are they?"

Sangshu pulled out her comscreen, opened it to a message from Copper. It was a moving image of Mother and Father, along with Chuiliu and Changqing, and with them were Cogs as well, all carried by the wind, away from the Palace, heading back to Feng.

A breath of relief stuttered from my lips and Sangshu returned her comscreen to the folds of her robes.

I was no longer bound to Fog by duty—by fear. Yet now, even as I was free to make my own choices, conflict brewed within.

18

SANGSHU
A WAITING ERUPTION DORMANT

"You don't know... do you?" I asked my eldest sister. I watched the storm churning in her expression as she took in the destruction around us—the pieces of Engine falling, the parts still desperately holding together, the Natural Engines and Titans colliding to destroy, to repair, working with, against, one another in a clash of wind and waves. All of it muffled into the background as I stared, unwaveringly, at Lufeng before turning again, angling myself instead towards time falling like a river from the sky.

"Have you ever wondered why Grandmother rarely left Feng herself? And never for long? And never far?" I asked. Our arguments growing up had never been loud, rather, they were fought wordlessly. Lufeng didn't respond.

Silence. Stillness.

Something I once found solace in.

I blew out a long exhale of steam and smoke. "She can't," I said. "Unless she dies."

Silence. Stillness.

Even as the world around us shook and remained shaking.

I continued to speak as though the two of us were standing back in Feng, in the rain bloom fields, where there was a true quiet I'd forgotten I'd once longed for each day. "Because her roots are so tangled, so deeply buried in Feng that they can know no other soil. But her roots reach so much farther than that... to Glace, to... Engine. And if she dies, all else dies with her, and if all else dies... she, too, dies, with them..."

I fell silent and there was a long pause.

Finally, Lufeng spoke again, quietly, eyes wide, horrified, her pupils narrowed to pricks so small they almost disappeared altogether. "I did not know."

"You cannot know everything, but you can leverage what you do know and sometimes that simply has to be enough," I said. "That is what I've done, that is what I've been doing. That is why I'm here. Why I'm trying to save this wretched place that I'd come to unwillingly realize is so precious to the Cogs, just as Feng is to us, Glace is to Exile Song."

Then, "You learn fast when there isn't time to learn."

"Do you think that was why we never learned in

Feng? Because we had too much time?" Her response surprised me. Grandmother would've voiced a similar sentiment.

I smiled, wondering if it might be one of the last times I had the chance to do so and wished I had thought to seek out more things that brought me joy, the way observing in silence in Feng had, the way studying alchemy had, the way watching the slow sway of rain blooms used to, the way Exile Song—

"Perhaps. Or perhaps it was because we never felt the need to."

I turned and marveled at Lufeng's long needle threads, a grove of tresses that no longer sat upon the crown of my own head. Lufeng's eyes roamed my transformed body, searching and seemingly failing to find something familiar in my changed features.

Her voice became distant once more. "Have you seen what they've done to our family? To the other Wind Walkers and Water Shifters. What exists on Gear—"

I thought, too, of Engine itself, what rested within its core, Blinking Star and the others. Knowing this would only further enrage Lufeng. It seemed like, to Lufeng, much like to the rebels, losing everything was worth it to sate their desire for vengeance that had been left to fester, run rampant, like the corroveins plaguing the body of the iron giant.

Father and our sisters may have been wearing shells, but they couldn't change the dead hearts resting within them that were incapable of decay. They were not true products of the alchemy of flesh, not fusions of Natural Engines nor the new race of Natural Titans. But that wasn't something to be brought up now. Lufeng would continue to believe what she already held true.

It felt almost arrogant of me to think of my sister as ignorant, but Gear and Engine did that—make people arrogant, make them believe they were superior in what they knew or thought they knew and understood, even though they were proven wrong just as quickly and easily within not minutes but seconds. I, too, had allowed that arrogance to touch me. Everyone held their opinions as though theirs could only ever be the soundest of truths.

I bowed my head, its hanging weight an anchor threatening to capsize the already sinking Treader that was my mind. It had been so obvious what my goal was at the beginning, but now, I wasn't sure. Would it be better to allow Engine to fall? To allow Grandmother and all else to fall with it?

"Did you know they call us gods here? Those natural gods we ourselves had always referred to, do you know why we never see them? Because we *are* them. The retaliation of the natural gods is what they believe this is." I gestured to the corroveins. "Divine punishment."

"They chose this first." But even as she said the words, her voice wavered, and I clutched on fast to it.

"We don't have to choose the same."

I had once wanted to destroy Engine, crumple it beneath my alchemy. But it was no longer just Engine: Zinc and his ancestors' creation. It was also a part of Grandmother, interconnected to Feng, to Glace. And it was also a home to many who wouldn't have one otherwise. And it didn't have to be built upon death. There was always another choice. All our homes could survive, *Grandmother*, too, could also survive.

Lufeng considered me briefly, her expression torn. Then, that single moment was gone.

"So your choice stands? To let everything fall?" I asked.

"It seems to me everything has already fallen or will in the end." There was a firm edge to Lufeng's tone.

What I had told her about Grandmother only seemed to have further solidified her resolve.

Lufeng seemed so much like Grandmother as she stood in front of me now, and perhaps that was why Grandmother never told her the truth. She didn't need to. She understood Lufeng would make the same decision regardless. And Grandmother wanted her final fall to be at Lufeng's hands.

I couldn't stop my next words from leaving my lips even though I knew they were intended to ache, not just her but us both. "This is why Grandmother always loved you best."

She flinched, voice quiet as she murmured, "We will never be safe from them." She gathered wind around her. The conversation was drawing to an end, whether or not I had more to say. "I may not know as much as you, but I know who is most important to me, and what it is I am trying to protect, even if it means that the solution to that protection is death. I think you've lost sight of that, even if you believe otherwise. They will always have a new leader, and even if there are those of them who are kind-hearted, there will always be others who are not."

As she said this, it seemed as though she wanted me to continue to speak, to convince her of elsewise, and she seemed as tired as Grandmother, even though she was so much younger.

Lufeng's words continued to linger, and though there was pain, there was still tender affection etched in her wilted expression, something I never thought I'd see again: a tenderness that I thought had long left, an impossibility between us sisters now standing on opposing sides, causing within me a guilt that festered. My actions, though meant to mend, felt like bitter betrayal. And why did this betrayal feel so bitter even though I thought I was ready for it?

Even if we saved Engine, if Grandmother continued living, there may well be an endless cycle of destruction ongoing. Vicious. Chewing through our lives, the world, like rust spreading, eroding, flaking away what once held whole. And then what? It seemed an impossibility to break from such a cycle.

Instead of keeping things separate, perhaps what we needed was to bring them together, as they had been in the past, as they should be. I believed that had once been Grandmother's true intention, except she did not have enough knowledge for such a solution before she began losing faith in the possibility of such a future. Grandmother had immense wisdom, but only of her own people, the sphere of the part of the world she'd built alone, even though her roots stretched so much further. And as much as it was her virtue, it also became the undoing of our people.

I closed my eyes, knowing that this answer had always been in all of our hands, yet it was one held between fingers closed behind our backs, refusing to consider it as an option out of fear and worry. Because this was a solution with the most unpredictable, limitless conclusion; yet it was also one without a clear benefit to either the Cogs and Land Wanderers nor to the Wind Walkers and Water Shifters, and now, the Natural Titans as well.

There was always the worry of us making the same mistakes as those of the past, but we were not the same as those who came before us—at least, we did not have to be.

"I think I know the answer." I shook my head. "No, not the answer, but another option. A different choice than what has been offered us, than what we've all already chosen."

The wall would continue to remain an obstacle for all for as long as it stood.

Without another word, the two of us looked towards the Palace.

Lufeng had never seen where the wall ended, where it wrapped around Feng, Glace, Clay, because she never dared step outside of where she had been directed by others. Perhaps Grandmother had made it so she never strayed far, that none of us ever did, but Lufeng also chose to stay uncurious. Or perhaps, it was Grandmother herself who always feared stepping outside of Feng, and her fear echoed through us, generation after generation.

I thought of all the chambers for experimentation, the tools dedicated to further development of contraptions.

Lufeng looked back towards me, understanding dawning in her dark eyes.

To my surprise, Lufeng took my hand, and it shocked me how cold and rough it felt. Yet, it still brought me comfort. Then our attention shifted back to the wall that the Palace was encased within.

I was told by Copper that Grandmother had been the one who asked for the wall to be built—only she had no choice in what had been used to erect it.

Perhaps Grandmother asked for the wall to be built because she believed that to protect ourselves, we must keep ourselves unseen from the world. But what she didn't realize was that, perhaps, true armor took the form of being loud in our existence: allowing the world to hear the billow of our rushing winds, the roar of colliding waves, the irrepressible eruption that had lain dormant for far too long.

Revealing the reality of the two sides of the wall to one another, breaking down the divide Grandmother had sacrificed to erect, may result in chaos, massive disorder, crossovers that neither side was equipped or ready for—but perhaps that was what would finally end the cycle. But it was only one single possibility out of endless others, conclusions leading to greater failures than success.

"I don't know how this will end," I said, eyes unmoving from the long stretch of the seemingly infallible wall, extending so far upwards that it appeared as though it were a part of the sky.

"You don't have to know everything, isn't that right?" Lufeng smiled.

If they refused to open the doors of their minds, then we must create a new passage.

But sometimes having a perceived boundless freedom was just as dangerous as being under total control without a single breath of agency, or perhaps…

Whether or not this was the correct choice—if any choice could be considered truly correct—there was never meant to be a wall, and so of course we must cause its fall, if there was anything that should be falling, so there might be hope that rises once more from its ashes.

19

SANGSHU
A PALACE NEAR THE WIND

I want to tell you of a different conversation I had with the Buried Engine—

I—

Protection and control—is there a difference between the two? You'd kept all of us hidden for so long yet let us leave one by one, knowing what the other side of the wall held for us.

She—

I cannot protect those who do not wish to be protected.

I—

But they didn't know.
What if they wished to return?

She—

Then they would, will.

I—

What if they cannot?

She—

Child, you may see me and think of me
as powerful, but I cannot save everyone,
not when I can barely save myself.

I—

Did you know what the marriages truly
were when you agreed to send each of us away?

She—

Yes and no.

Script terms meant no more to me than
their promises. But I had to place my trust
in both because I had no other choice.

I—

You allowed them to take the bones

from our souls before they even had
a chance to return to the earth.

You sold all our freedom without asking,
what makes you any different from they?

She—

It does not.

I had to surrender to them to keep
what little is left of ourselves.

My child, I am tired.

I have been trying for endless cycles.

Centuries.

And we have only ever grown smaller.

Tell me.

What would you like me to do?

I am already falling.

I—

But you have not yet fallen.

She—

My roots are rotting.

I—

In my eyes, you are the tree
that never truly dies.

You are the wind that carries
Feng and the rest of us forth.

She—

I did not ask to be seen as
disaster nor as a god.

I had simply wished to be a quiet witness
of every passing breath that is given and taken
and disappear happy even if I am forgotten.

I had harbored the hopes of falling,
of resting, for a long, long time.

If that selfish of me?

Is it alright for me to fall?

Even if it meant that all
else would fall with me?

20

SANGSHU

AN ALCHEMY FOR HOPE

While studying alchemy, I'd discovered from the records within the library that the reason they were paving around the Palace towards Feng was because Zinc was attempting to hide what was buried beneath—the failures of alchemy that couldn't be thrown into the sea, for they would rise above the waves and serve as evidence of Zinc's incompetencies. At the same time, I'd learned of the true composition of the Palaces and the wall, and naturally, what it would take to cause its fall.

"Do you know why the wall is made of bone?" I reached a hand forth towards the iron giant as though I could touch the massive entity from such a distance.

The dead could not fall because they have already fallen. The decay of rust could not touch them. But

Lufeng was someone who also knew the answer and was quick to make the connection as she stared at my alchemized body, the smoke drifting from my hands, the serenity that no doubt sat in the resolved expression resting upon my face.

Instead of waiting for her answer, I pretended as though she'd already spoken as I whispered, "I am an alchemist of flesh."

But when I mustered the courage to look at my sister once more, she wasn't smiling.

She shook her head. "No."

But this time, we both understood she wasn't opposed to the solution itself, but what it would take to carry it through. I would need Lufeng's help because she was the wind that could fan the flames of the destruction I would sacrifice myself to become by unleashing the inferno tears I'd been holding dormant for too long. That would be the only way to collapse the wall, to expose it to a heat so great that the only thing it could do was crumble.

But, even with Lufeng's aid, I would only be able to crumble a small section, perhaps even a part of the Palace itself. For now, that would have to be enough.

It was as though the Buried Engine had heard my final choice, because something Grandmother had once told me drifted through the smoke within my mind. *You don't have to be the one to finish what you've started. It is all in the hands of those who come after.*

My mind had been focused on the collective to such an extent that I'd forgotten about all the individual lives—the one thing I promised myself I wouldn't do: believe each being was only another cog in the engine.

We are but cogs within the engine, but we need to believe that every single cog makes a difference, wouldn't you agree? came Copper's voice.

No matter how powerful we were or believed we were, it was impossible to cause change alone—yet the worse mistake was believing a single being's actions couldn't make a difference, just as the rebels believed a single being's actions were necessary for all the difference.

Zinc and the Cogs were so afraid of death, but not me, not us, not any more—because now I understood we were as dead as we were alive, and perhaps only acceptance of such a fact allowed me to feel truly alive, even knowing that I would soon be taking my final breaths.

I moved to stand face to face with Lufeng before lowering myself to one knee, the way I'd seen Taskers done to the Puppet Kings while they were unmounted from their Travelers, the same way guards kneeled before the Iron Alchemist.

No one said it had to be the phoenixes themselves who must die; sometimes it was only their flames.

May this be the one last thing I will do as your lacking sister. Please take care of the others for me when I'm gone, I whispered in my misted mind, already preparing itself for departure because I knew I had no right to make such a request of Lufeng after all.

"I am glad my sun will set to your wind."

Lufeng, hesitant to accept the fate I'd woven for myself, seemed as though she might take a step back before she stilled, then sighed, accepting my resolve by holding out a hand, asking me to rise.

Lufeng called upon the wind as we stood hand in hand, gazing towards the wall. Around us, the breeze churned, gathering us into its embrace and whisking us forth with an intensity that made it seem as though we were carried by the spirit of an ancient storm.

21

LUFENG

THE GUIDE AND THE GUIDED

I had once thought it was not possible to lose any more than I already had.

But of course, I did.

And I had once thought of returning home, to Feng, with Chuiliu, with Changqing, with Father, Mother, and every one of my sisters, but it seemed that this was never a dream possible, only a faint idealism now settled at the back of my mind.

This was not how I envisioned homecoming—the tearing down of the one thing I once believed was keeping us safe. And yet, looking at Sangshu now, as the wind embraced the two of us like a mother using her own body as shielding armor, bringing us together towards the Palace encased in the looming bone wall, I marveled at the way she was so willing to sacrifice herself.

Never the guide and always the guided. I almost laughed at the accuracy of her words now.

Yet this time, I did not mind.

22

SANGSHU

A RIVER FROM THE SKY

Grandmother was to become their first god, but she had been reduced to a hidden martyr still alive— They called her a tamed disaster, a smothered storm, a settled earthquake, a droughted flood, a stilled eruption, stifled wind—The Buried Engine.

It was ironic that this was the one thing that Zinc hadn't predicted. Lufeng and I noticed onyx watchers had gathered and were now following us from behind with an urgent sporadicity as we stormed through the sky from the summit of Engine towards the Palace and its encasing walls. From the collapsing gates of Engine below came thundering Travelers, and Treaders beneath, all with guards settled atop, chasing us towards the walls. I didn't allow myself to dwell, to relish for too long in the nectar of this first victory against the Iron Alchemist who seemed impossible to rattle.

It seemed our presence did not go unnoticed by Exile Song, Copper, Elder Yinxing, or the other Natural Engines and Titans, because as soon as they deciphered our objective, they broke from their stations in surges to chase the guards after us across the bridges, leaving the rebels in stunned confusion.

With the wall quickly approaching ahead, I turned to my sister.

"Lufeng."

"Yes?"

"I give you permission to tell me that I was wrong," I sputtered, hoping the wind didn't muffle my words. I wouldn't repeat them.

"About what?"

"Everything."

She laughed, the sound so effortless and carefree. Sometimes she could be so childlike, and I wondered if this was the first time she felt as though she were allowed to behave as such, because for a moment she'd had the weight taken off her shoulders and placed onto mine, even though she knew it would fall upon hers once more. I allowed the lingering sound of her laughter to wrap around me like ticklish caresses. Then I shouted for Lufeng to place me atop the wall, not too close to the farthest edge of the Palace encased in it, because I was sure if I held onto her, leaned into her wind, for a moment longer, I may not let go.

As soon as she deposited me, she worked on pushing back the swarming onyx watchers. Wind swirled around her, propelled forward by her hands in eager gusts, firm rather than violent. Below, guards on Travelers spilled from the Palace, talons scraping against the wall, defying gravity the way birds would while in flight. It seemed not everyone had evacuated, but it was evident why. There were many who were willing to die with their home.

In the distance were the rebels, following Copper's Engines and Titans closely. They, too, abandoned their stations: it was almost jarring the way the corroveins immediately halted in their growth. My only hope was that neither the rebels or Zinc and his guards would reach Lufeng and I before we shattered the wall and the Palace, or what we could of it.

I closed my eyes, focusing on the inferno tears within me, my alchemy-made core, a thing that had seemed so uncontrollable when I first stepped out of the Iron Alchemist's chamber, one I thought would unleash as soon as I opened my eyes, tried to speak, and yet, I was able to learn how to contain it, until now. I allowed each fissure and crevice along the shell of my body to exhale and with it the release of a blistering heat hotter than any fire.

I was disrupted by a sudden cry from Lufeng.

My eyes flew open, but instead of what I anticipated—Lufeng spiraling towards the sea—the Natural Titans in the form of Currents brewed up curtains of heavy fog, disorientating the vision of guards on Travelers climbing up the sides of the wall, claws now fumbling against the grainy surface with metallic squeals, some bumping into one another in their tightly packed formations.

Darting up the wall with the help of Wind Walkers was Exile Song, in staccato bursts as he knocked guard after guard off their Travelers. His expression was unsettled, almost desperate, whereas I'd always only seen him calm. Next to him Copper, on another Traveler, threw several guards off-balance in her path towards us. On her face was an expression of maternal worry: when was the last time I'd seen such an emotion? Several of the machines halted and tumbled downwards without their operators, others continued without a single stutter upwards alone. Below, Wind Walkers pillowed the falls of the guards so they landed softly on the ground, disorientated but unharmed less for the shock of an almost-death.

Surrounding Exile Song and Copper in all directions was a slowly collecting mass of Natural Engines and Titans, both rebels and non-rebels alike. The sight revealed how no one truly held any power at all when the collective realized how easily it was to take it out of the singular's hands. The gods Zinc had thought he already controlled ran wild and rampant and brought to life his worst fear rather than his long-awaited dreams. It was a glorious sight—the uncontrolled, the unpredictable, the once unimaginable. But I also had to thank Zinc, because I would not know of alchemy elsewise, even though it had resulted in consequences in the wake of its curious creations.

When Exile Song reached the top of the wall, following close behind, making themselves known when they must have been previously hidden between Engines and Currents, were Blinking Star and the other Sun Cores. Copper lingered at the back of the group, watching with weary understanding. I was glad Blinking Star and the others had been able to successfully break free from the confines of Engine's heat chambers. I hoped Nickel, and those like them who had a hand in their release—the brave show of their defiance, their courage to stand against Zinc for those they had been told to fear and smother—had found safety either below ground or away from Engine. I hoped what we were trying to accomplish now might only foster in them further confidence that *this* was all worth it.

"You knew," I said to Exile Song, voice barely a whisper, "that I would make this choice."

"Does anyone know you better?" His body was once again devoid of oric. Transmutation was already a difficult, almost impossible feat, and reverse transmutation was unheard of. If there was one other alchemist Zinc feared other than me, it was Exile Song, who had learned in secret as a guard, from watching alone.

"Always remain—"

"—one step ahead." Exile Song bowed his head. "Even if I didn't know your final choice, I have faith in every single decision you have ever made," he continued.

"Even the mistakes?" I asked, quiet.

"Even the mistakes." Then, "Is it cruel of me to say that you sometimes remind me of him?"

A laugh escaped me. "Is it cruel of me to say the same of you?"

We shared a smile.

Then Exile Song looked down at the space between us, but before he could speak again, I asked, "Why are you loyal to me?"

He hummed, the sound like the sea mourning a recent loss. "Because you aren't confined to what you think you know and understand," he said. "Because you're not afraid to sacrifice yourself for something greater, even if it means you won't be remembered."

I stared at him, then shook my head. "I will be."

Exile Song's gentle smile became desolate, and I was sure my own expression mirrored his.

Blinking Star startled me when she took hold of my hand in both awe and disbelief. The other Sun Cores mimicked her action, taking one another's hands. In a line, we almost resembled various phases of a sun in the stages of an eclipse.

"It seems I am being offered aid I don't deserve," I whispered.

But the world had always deserved this—freedom. And they, the Sun Cores, too, release.

"We didn't want to, nor had the courage to admit that we were dying, that we were already dead, but you saved us from our final moments of defeat and gave us a new reason to live. For that, I never had the chance to thank you," Blinking Star said with a small smile. "Let me, all of us, return to you the second life you've given us."

Next to me, close but not touching, stood Exile Song, with an expression of desolate defeat. I had never been afraid of loss, never truly, until I met him, and I had never been afraid of death, never truly, until this moment. In the distance, I spot Copper, silent tears trailing down her cheeks. We worked together, yet we had never grown close, never truly, not the way I had with Zinc in the past, and yet we had developed a quiet bond that was intimate in its own way, and I knew this was a loss that would linger, for us both.

I allowed myself tears for the last time and wondered if I would burn long enough to watch the wall fall—

As my eyes shut once more, the inferno tears were an awaiting eruption that were quick in their outburst, splitting the crevices of my shell, tearing me from within, like flesh shredding layer by layer. The heat seared, swallowed, subsumed, and as soon as it made its final escape, I opened my eyes to watch Blinking Star be the first to alight next to me—one by one, each Sun Core glowed amber, like candles touched by the flick of the tongue of a leaping flame hungry for destruction, for flesh, blood, bones, gnawing until there was nothing left of the world but a carcass, but instead of one gleaming, white and smooth, so stripped of muscle, organ, flesh, skin that it cannot hope to even rot in its utter defiance, it left a burning inferno Lufeng and the other gathered Wind Walkers carried down the walls, disintegrating all the Travelers now empty of guards in its wake.

Soon, the wall began to collapse right beneath us, and we began to fall with it, crumble with it, turn to ashes with it.

—And I did.

For a moment.

A glimpse.

It was almost illogical how little had changed while Engine and Gear seemed to undergo entire transformations with each passing annual I'd seen, both during my time here and from what had been recorded in both Script and images in the library.

I'd forgotten truly just how slowly time moved on the other side of the wall, where Feng and Glace lay, almost like a meandering conversation, the way the wind carried a message to another, and sometimes the message reached its intended receiver after the immediacy of its importance. But perhaps that was why Wind Walkers were able to let so many things go, knowing how little it all mattered in the grandness of the world and within a seemingly timeless and immortal realm.

As I closed my eyes once more to the fall of all our ashes, mixed with the walls' crumbling, brittle bones, I realized this was what the Buried Engine foresaw—her own death.

I had always, from the beginning, wanted to go quietly like Grandmother. But I suppose that was impossible from the moment I touched alchemy, reached for death, and let go of the wind's guiding hand.

Still, I found myself smiling, regretting none of it—none of it at all.

The embrace of the spirit of the ancient storm around Lufeng left at the same moment the sun tear fell, draining me entirely from each fissure pried open, and the last thing I felt from within was Exile Song's true name—

23

LUFENG

A SUN SETTING IN ASH

The Cogs—at least the ones who did not rush to our aid—the disorientated guards, Zinc, were all nowhere to be found, but there was no doubt we would see them again. But for now, my focus was on the wall crumbling down, that carried the eruptions of my sister and her creations in a river of ash from the sky, drifting towards unchanging Feng, ever storming Glace.

Sangshu was gone, along with the setting sun in the bleeding skies, when the falling cinders found rest on the upturned soil, half-tilled, leading towards our home.

Among the ashes of bones scattered at the bottom of the crumbled section of the wall, I held what remained of my sister. Within my palm nestled a brilliant orb of amber, emitting from its body a cooling inferno that I knew would burn once more. Just like for Sangshu, for us all, for the revolution upon us that had been long brewing and would continue to persist, could not be defined by this single moment in our near immortal lives—there was no such thing as a true end, because change was cyclical, like the sun, it was something that rose and set and rose again.

Where the left side of the Palace used to be was now a gaping maw, gazing outwards to a place those of Engine had only heard of but never truly experienced. Behind me, waves crashed against the cliffs, the sound of their recession like a wash of showering rain, and for a moment I wondered how it might feel to fall towards the piercing peaks waiting below, this time without anyone to catch me, without anyone falling with me, and I wondered if that was how Sangshu felt at the very end. Alone. Or did she feel the warmth she sought and gained and lost again?

Back in Feng, out of us all, Sangshu was most like the wind, someone who came and went, came and went, came and went, never loud in her entrance nor exit—without a word nor a single whisper.

Staring at her now, I knew what it was her ashes reminded me of—the seeds of seeking rain blooms. She had certainly helped more than one find what they sought.

I placed her amid the ashes that swallowed the core

like dim clouds, yet speckles of amber and glistening bright white continued to peek through the dull cinder like leaking tears.

From the first moment I saw her in her alchemized form, Sangshu resembled a sun waiting to set.

Now, she was waiting no longer.

But to my surprise, a hand reached out and pulled Sangshu's core from the ashes, the heat sizzling against the rippling water of his skin, steam drifting from the contact against flesh. There was no pain in his expression, only a tender longing, a droughting river waiting for rain.

"She told me she wanted to visit Glace someday," Exile Song said. "And I told her I'd take her." Then, without another word, the Water Shifter crossed the glorious chasm where the wall once stood, seemingly drifting in the direction of his home, which remained a long way's journey, until the ashes churned up by the wind that quietly followed from behind carried him from sight.

I stared towards Feng, the waiting trees, the families new and old resting in the embrace of hollows, and smiled.

It was time for me to return home, too.

EPILOGUE
EXILE SONG

I want to tell you about when I first learned of Exile Song's true name—

It is not the buildup, but the peak of release, the eruption of water and steam, one that cannot be put in Script, nor Breath, only the deep murmurs of Song.

I remember asking him once—

What is a heart and a
heartbeat to a Water Shifter?

Him—

We do not have a Cog equivalent,
if that is what you're asking.

I—

I see.

Him—

What about for those of Feng?

I—

*It's humorous, when I voice it aloud
really, because we do have hearts, but
our hearts are dead but do not decay.*

Could you consider that immortal?

Or perhaps spectral is more accurate...

*Perhaps it is the Water Shifters who are
the true immortals, since you don't have
hearts that can stop nor be taken away.*

Him—

Immortal...

*Maybe it is precise to say that we
are... regenerative, even if we do not
leave and return in the same form
we entered in, just like the wind.*

I—

Just like the wind...

AFTERWORD

We ask the stars, *Are there other living beings; is there somewhere else we can live*? But we do not ask the earth, *How can we keep you alive*?

As I was writing *A River from the Sky,* I thought much about how things are lost when transported and translated, taken out of the natural context of their culture and people and community. Even when it is carried by someone of their culture, bits of it will flake, scatter behind like breadcrumbs, fragments nestled in the indent of footprints fading. And sometimes, it is only a shard that remains when the carrier reaches their destination, or finally finds the will or courage to raise what they have been travelling with in their hands and hearts—even if broken, with pieces of it left behind, a person half whole, waiting to reunite with another half, yet no longer remembering what that half looks like, nor where they might be able to find it, if ever.

I thought about the way humans colonize nature, the way humans colonize their own kind. Where peace walks on the fine line of contracts, agreements, flimsy pieces of paper and hard-to-understand legal jargon. Of forced submission, of unknowing submission, simply because we know no better. To bow without knowing why we're bowing. You may think you don't, but at least once in your life you have done so, both consciously or unconsciously—physically or mentally—to someone, to something.

When people say the answer is simple—*Yes or no. This or that*—it never is simple.

To all those who have been displaced, have become unwilling migrants, this is for you.

ACKNOWLEDGMENTS

There are so many people I have to thank in helping me wrap up the first duology I've ever written—Cath, Bahar, Elora, Kate, and the entire Titan Books team; Lisa who had championed the series; Nat for the gorgeous cover; Nancy and David for the lovely preorder art; those who read an earlier version of the book, Leah, Mai, Zana; my family and spouse always for their support and belief in me; to Focus, my spouse, again for making sure I'm always hydrated and fed when I go into hyper-focus mode when I'm actively drafting and editing, when I essentially disappear from the world for a week or two—sometimes longer; and to all the readers and reviewers and booksellers, everyone who have supported, have been supporting, and continue to support me and my career—I wouldn't be here without you all.

ABOUT THE AUTHOR

Ai Jiang is a Chinese-Canadian writer, Ignyte, Bram Stoker®, and Nebula Award winner, and Hugo, Astounding, Locus, Aurora and BSFA Award finalist born in Changle, Fujian, currently residing in Markham, Ontario. Her work can be found in F&SF, The Dark, Clarkesworld, and The Masters Review, among others. She is the author of *A Palace Near the Wind, Linghun* and *I AM AI*. Find her at www.aijiang.ca.